"You rea **splattered with a fresh load of mud?"**

"I don't care," Molly declared.

"I do," Dan replied.

"Why?" she said, a strange flutter breezing over her.

He reached out and cupped his palm against the side of her neck. "Because I care about you, whether or not you believe me. And right now you need me."

She'd needed him for years! He was the reason she'd never found passion with another man. He was the cause of all those sleepless nights, all those secret tears. But she'd rather die than tell him so. "No, I don't," she said, shying away. "I'm used to coping on my own."

"It's okay to ask for help, Molly. We all need other people some of the time."

"Except you."

INTERNATIONAL DOCTORS

They're guaranteed to raise your pulse!

Look for the newest title
in this new series.

The Passion Treatment
by
Kim Lawrence
#2330

Available only from

Harlequin Presents®

Catherine Spencer

THE DOCTOR'S SECRET CHILD

INTERNATIONAL
DOCTORS

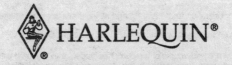

HARLEQUIN®

TORONTO • NEW YORK • LONDON
AMSTERDAM • PARIS • SYDNEY • HAMBURG
STOCKHOLM • ATHENS • TOKYO • MILAN • MADRID
PRAGUE • WARSAW • BUDAPEST • AUCKLAND

ISBN 0-373-12311-6

THE DOCTOR'S SECRET CHILD

First North American Publication 2003.

Visit us at www.eHarlequin.com

Printed in U.S.A.

CHAPTER ONE

THE house looked smaller, poorer even, than she remembered, but the dark blue sedan parked on the snowplowed road in front was new and expensive. Still, never for a moment would Molly have expected it would belong to Dan Cordell. It was too conservative, too practical. Not his sort of accessory at all. He was the Harley kind—hell on two wheels and the devil be damned.

The voice that greeted her as she swung open her mother's front door, though, was exactly his: dark and smooth as black silk. "So you finally deigned to come back," he said.

Molly wondered if the shock she felt ravaged her face as mercilessly as it violated her body. "Of course I did," she said, clutching the door knob desperately in the hope that its cheap metal digging coldly into her palm would distract her from the painful lurch of her heart. "My mother, I'm told, has been injured and needs someone to help her recuperate, so there was never any question but that I'd come back."

He shrugged, as though he didn't believe her, and nodded at Ariel. "And she...?"

Molly had known it was a question she'd have to answer, but not so soon and never to him. *He* must never guess. "Is my daughter."

"That much I already figured out." Just a trace of the smile which, once, had lured her to forget every sense of decency her puritanical father had tried so hard to instill in her, touched his mouth. "What I was going to ask is, what's her name?"

"Ariel," she said, drawing her beloved child closer, as if doing so would protect her from ever having to know the truth of who *he* really was.

His gaze, as startlingly blue and direct as ever but softened now with a compassion it hadn't possessed eleven years before, settled on Ariel. "It's a very pretty name," he allowed. "Just like its owner."

Though Ariel smiled with pure delight, fear pinched Molly's heart. What if her own searching for a trace of those aristocratic Cordell genes hadn't been as thorough or impartial as she liked to think, and he saw in the child a resemblance to himself which Molly had missed? What if some sort of preternatural flash of insight told him he'd just met his own flesh and blood?

Before he could make the connection, she pushed Ariel toward the kitchen at the end of the narrow hall. "Go see what's in the refrigerator, sweetheart. We might need to make a run to the corner store before we do anything else. Look for milk and bread and eggs and juice—you know, the kind of thing we always have on hand at home."

He watched Ariel's long legs cover the distance and Molly braced herself, sure unkind destiny had finally caught up with her. But, "I didn't know you'd be bringing your family with you, Molly," was all he said, shrugging into the sheepskin-lined denim jacket he'd flung over the coat stand.

"And I didn't know you had a key to my mother's house," she replied sharply, the rush of adrenaline inspired by fear seeking escape in outrage. "Or did you break in?"

As if her finding him there to begin with hadn't been shock enough, he answered, "I'm your mother's doctor, and old-fashioned enough to believe in making house calls.''

Molly's mouth fell open. Dan Cordell, whose chief pastime eleven years ago had been trolling for women and collecting more speeding tickets than any other well-to-do layabout in town, a *doctor? Old-fashioned?* ''Of course you are!'' she scoffed, taking in his blue jeans and off-white fisherman's knit sweater. ''And I'm Anna, former governess to the King of Siam's many children.''

''On the contrary, Molly. You're the absentee daughter so ashamed of her parents that she chose to forget they existed once she hooked up with a rich husband, so let's not try to confuse truth with fantasy.''

He could dish out insults as easily as he'd once doled out charm. The chill of his disapproval cast an even longer shadow than that of his six-foot-three-inch frame backlit by the cold mid-March sun filtering weakly through the window behind him. But it lost something of its sting with his reference to her marital status.

Caught between a burst of hysterical laughter and outright scorn, she almost squeaked, *Rich husband? Who thought up that fairy tale?* but brought herself under control enough to reply coolly, ''Let's not indeed! Assuming you're telling the truth for once and really are her doctor, how do you rate my mother's condition?''

''Poorly enough that I don't want her trying to move around without assistance. A fall out of bed or down those steep stairs could finish her off. Even before the accident, she was in bad shape.''

''Bad shape how?''

He subjected Molly to a brief, clinical inspection, sweeping his glance from her glove-soft leather boots to the cashmere sweater showing above the fur-trimmed collar of her coat. "I find it depressing that you even have to ask. If you—"

"If I weren't such a pitiful excuse for a daughter, I'd already know why," she cut in. "Well, don't let the clothes fool you, *Doctor!* Underneath, I'm still that shameless, unruly Paget girl whose parents deserved better than to be saddled with a child marked by the devil."

"Those are your words, Molly, not mine."

"They are the words which drove me out of town before I turned eighteen, and they were whispered loudly enough for everyone to hear. I imagine they'll find new life now that I've returned."

"Is that why you stayed away all these years? Because you felt you didn't belong?"

She bit back a sigh, unwilling—*unable*—to tell him the truth: that after he'd grown tired of her and their clandestine summer fling, she discovered she was pregnant; that she was afraid her father would half-kill her if he found out; that she had no one to turn to because her mother hadn't had the courage to defy her husband's iron-fisted rule and help her. And that she hated all of them for what it had cost her.

"Never mind me," she said. "I asked you about my mother. I know my parents' car was hit by a train at a railroad crossing, that my father was killed instantly and my mother left seriously injured. I'd like to know the extent of those injuries and if she'll recover from them."

Something flickered in Dan's eyes, a fleeting expression almost like regret. "You've changed, Molly. You're nothing like the girl I used to know."

"I certainly hope not!"

"You've lost your sweetness."

"I've lost my juvenile illusions, Doctor. And if you're still hanging on to yours, I'm not sure you're fit to be in charge of my mother's care. Which brings up another point: why isn't your father taking care of my mother? He's been our family doctor for as far back as I can remember.''

"He retired last year, so if it's a second medical opinion you're after, you won't get it from him. But I'll be happy to refer you to someone else, though if it's a specialist you're after, it'll mean looking farther afield than Harmony Cove. I've already consulted the only orthopedic surgeon and respirologist in town, and both concur with my lowly family practitioner's opinion.''

"I just might do that." She tapped her booted foot on the worn linoleum and hoped he'd read it as a sign of impatience rather than the nervousness it really depicted. When she'd heard that Dr. Cordell had suggested social services contact her, it had never occurred to her that it was the son who'd assumed the mantle of medical expertise, and the idea took some getting used to. "Meanwhile, I'd appreciate a straight answer to a question you seem anxious to sidestep. How is my mother—and don't bother to sugarcoat your reply. If she's not going to recover or she's likely to be left a permanent invalid, say so.''

His mouth, which once had inspired her to a passion so all-consuming that even now, eleven years later, the memory still sent a flush of heat through her belly, tightened grimly. "Prolonged use of steroids to treat her asthma have left her with secondary osteoporosis. Couple this with age, poor diet and general disregard for the maintenance of good health, and you're looking at a woman whose ribs are so fragile that too energetic a hug could, quite literally, prove bone-crushing. The impact from the collision left her with a fractured hip which is being held together by surgically implanted steel pins. It's possible she'll become ambulatory again. It's unlikely she'll do so without the aid of a walker. It's possible her bone health can be improved, but only marginally and *only* if she takes her prescribed medications. But she's forgetful and depressed. I don't think she's particularly interested in getting well. I'd even go so far as to say she wants to die. Is that direct enough for you, Molly?''

Direct enough? Dear heaven, she was quivering inside from an up swell of shock and pain so acute they almost cost her her self-control. A great bubble of grief rose in her throat, as unexpected as it was inappropriate. ''Quite,'' she said, and yanked open the front door. The cold Atlantic wind slapped her in the face and she welcomed it. It restored her faster than any amount of tea or sympathy. ''Thank you for stopping by.''

He took his time doing up his jacket and closing his black leather medical bag. ''Your eagerness to see the back of me is premature, my dear. I want to be sure you understand your mother's limitations and have some idea how to keep her comfortable before I turn her over to your tender mercies.''

She swept him a scornful glance. ''The social worker who contacted me gave a very thorough picture of what to expect. I hardly need a prescription to change linen or empty a bedpan.''

''I doubt you're as well-prepared as you think. It's been years since you saw your mother, and you're going to be shocked at the change in her. You might want to have me stick around for moral support, if nothing else.''

''No. I prefer to assess her state of mind and body without your breathing down my neck the whole time, so unless there's specific medication or treatment—?''

''Both,'' he said, ''but the public health nurse stops by twice a day to take care of all that.''

"Then if I have any other questions, I'll speak with you—or another doctor—later in the week."

He regarded her levelly a moment. "You'll have questions, Molly, make no mistake about that. And until or unless your *mother* elects to have someone else take over her case, you'll address them to me. Furthermore, you'll do it tomorrow. Make an appointment for midmorning. I'm not in my father's old office. You'll find me in the Eastside Clinic, down on Waverley Street, next to the old seamen's union building. Cadie Boudelet from next door will sit with Hilda while you're gone."

"What makes you so sure you know Cadie Boudelet will make herself available? She and my mother were never that close in the old days."

"Because she's practically been living here ever since Hilda was discharged from the hospital."

"She must have her hands full, doing that *and* minding everyone else's business!"

"Well, someone had to step in and act the Good Samaritan, and you didn't seem in any particular hurry to volunteer for the job."

She closed her eyes because she couldn't bear the censure she saw in his. When she opened them again, he was striding down the path, his shoulders bent into the wind, his dark head flecked with snowflakes. Not sparing her another glance, he climbed into his car, and drove down the hill toward the harbor.

From where she stood, Molly could see the lobster traps stacked by the sheds, and one or two hardy souls repairing fishing nets spread out on the paved area next to the docks. In another three months the snow would be gone and spring would color the scene in softer hues. The tourists would arrive in droves to exclaim over the picturesque sight of the lighthouse on the rocks jutting out at the end

of the quay, and the petunias spilling down to meet the
pavement from flower boxes nailed to the side of the
wooden lobster shack.

Strangers would click their cameras and run their video
film, and tell each other Harmony Cove was the prettiest
darn town on the eastern seaboard. But right now, the
entire scene was overlaid with gray misery relieved only
by a slick of newly fallen snow on the steeply sloping
roofs of the little houses lining the street.

She hated every last miserable stick and stone of the
place. They brought back too vivid a reminder of the people who lived inside those houses—of their narrow-
minded, judgmental outlook, their willingness to believe
the worst of others, their certainty that the way they'd
done things for the last hundred or more years was the
only way, and that *they* were right and anyone who
thought or acted differently was wrong.

Closing the door, she turned back to the hall just as
Ariel came out of the kitchen. "We don't need to go
shopping, Mommy. The refrigerator's full of food."

"Maybe, but most of it's probably been sitting there
for weeks and should be thrown out."

"No. The milk and eggs are fresh. I looked at the date
on the cartons."

If she said it was so, it was. Ariel might be only ten
and still a little girl in most respects, but having only one
parent had forced responsibility on her a lot sooner than
other children her age. She'd been just four the first time
she'd said, *Don't forget we have to take out the garbage
today, Mommy.* Sometimes, when things went wrong—
and it happened often in those early years—Ariel had
stepped into the role of comforter as easily as if she, and
not Molly, were the parent.

Remembering, Molly tweaked one of her daughter's

long dark braids and held out her hand for a high five. "You're such a little woman! What would I do without you?"

It was a question she asked often but today, for the first time, it took on somber new meaning. If Dan ever learned the truth and took Ariel away from her, how *would* she go on living?

Pushing aside the thought because it simply was not to be entertained, she tucked an arm around the child's waist. "Let's take your bag upstairs and go say hello to your grandmother. Maybe meeting you for the first time will cheer her up."

The stairs loomed ahead, dark and steep, evoking in Molly memories of being banished to her tiny room when she was even younger than Ariel. The house had seemed full of threatening shadows then; of hidden monsters waiting to leap out and punish her for sins she never fully understood. Now, perhaps for the first time, she saw the place for what it really was: a desperately stark box as severe and confining as the man who'd once ruled it with an iron fist.

The door to her parents' room door stood ajar. Pushing it wider, Molly peered inside and was immediately swallowed in another blast from the past. The same plain brown linoleum covered the floor. The thin beige curtains at the window were as familiar as the black iron bedstead hulking in the corner with a plain wooden cross hanging above it, on the wall.

Never had her father carried her from her own bed and snuggled her between him and her mother to chase away a bad dream. Not once had she been invited to climb in beside them for a morning cuddle or a nighttime story. In her child's mind, that room had been as spartan as a prison cell, and looking at it now through an adult's eyes, she saw nothing to change that perspective.

Aware that she was no longer alone, the woman half-reclining against the pillow shifted, raised one flannel-clad arm weakly, then let it flop down again. "Cadie, is that you?"

Shocked by the feeble voice, Molly stepped closer and saw that Dan had not exaggerated. Hilda Paget had never been a big woman but injury, illness, and a lifetime of hardship had reduced her to little more than a bag of fragile bones held together by loose skin.

Blinded by a wash of grief and guilt beside which the years of resentment and anger seemed suddenly pointless, she said, "No, Mom, it's me."

"*Molly?*" Again, the woman moved, this time trying to lean forward, but the effort cost her dearly and she sank back with a grunt of pain. But her eyes burned holes in her sunken face. "Child, you shouldn't have come! People will start talking all over again."

Swallowing the sudden lump in her throat, Molly bent to press a kiss on her mother's cheek and stroked the limp hair away from her brow. "Let them. I'm here to take care of you, and that's the only thing that matters."

"But I already have someone. The nurse comes by twice a day, and Cadie from next door stops in every morning and again at night, and does a bit of shopping when I need it. And Alice Livingston brings me soup at noon." But despite her protests, she clutched at Molly's hands as if she never wanted to let go. "How did you know I was in trouble, Moll? Who told you?"

"The hospital social worker, abetted by your new doctor. Why weren't you the one to call me, Momma? Did you think I wouldn't care that you've been hurt or that I'd turn my back on you when you needed help?"

"I knew how much you hated it here, and what it would cost you to come back again."

"I still hate it here. I probably always will."

"Then why put yourself out for a woman who never looked out for you the way a mother should?"

"Because you *are* still my mother, and now that my father's gone…"

She didn't finish the sentence; didn't add, "there's nothing to keep me away," because there was no need to hammer the point home. John Paget had chased her from the house so often, wielding whatever came to hand and cursing her at the top of his lungs the entire time, that there wasn't a soul in that dismal neighborhood who didn't know how deep and abiding the antagonism between father and daughter had been.

Many was the hour she'd shivered in the bitter winter cold, with nothing but hand-knit slippers on her feet and a thin sweater to protect her from the wind and the snow; many the summer night that she'd hidden in the wood shed behind the house until she'd deemed it safe to venture to her room again.

Yet for all that people had seen and heard, they'd shown her not a shred of pity. Instead they'd stood in their doorways and shaken their sanctimonious heads as yet another family fight erupted into the street. *Poor John Paget, plagued with such a hussy, and him with only one leg, poor soul! Wild, that's what she is. Born that way and she'll die that way. Tsk!*

No doubt when they heard she was back, they'd lurk around the cemetery, waiting to catch her dancing on his grave. As if she'd expend the energy! She was glad he was dead, and if anyone asked, she wouldn't compromise her integrity by denying it. He'd been a monster and the world was well rid of him.

"Don't think I haven't paid for what I let happen when you were little," Hilda Paget said, the suffering in her eyes provoked by hurts which went deeper than those afflicting her broken body. "It's haunted me that I turned a blind eye to the way your father treated you. It would serve me right if you left me now to rot in this bed."

"What, and live down to everyone's worst expectations of me? Give them the chance to nod their heads and say, *I told you so?* Not likely!" Molly laughed, doing her best to make light of a past she couldn't change. "Sorry, Momma, but I'm here to stay for as long as you need me, and I haven't come alone."

Her mother's glance flickered to Ariel hovering near the door. Her voice broke. "You brought your little girl to visit me? Oh, Moll, I never thought to see the day!"

The yearning in her mother's eyes, the pathetic gratitude in her voice, ripped holes in Molly's heart. Steeling herself against the onslaught of emotion, because she knew Ariel would dissolve into tears if she saw her mother was upset, she beckoned to the child. "Come and be introduced, sweetheart."

With more composure than any ten-year-old had a right to possess, Ariel came to lean lightly against the side of the bed. "Hello, Grandma. I'm sorry you got hurt when your car was hit by a train."

Tears pooled in Hilda's eyes. "Dear Lord!" she quavered, wrapping her bony fingers around Ariel's small hand. "Dear Lord, you take me back near eighteen years! You're the image of your momma when she was your age, child, the living image. So pretty, so fine. Look at those big brown eyes and that lovely hair, Moll! She's all of you, and nothing of me, thank God!"

What she didn't come right out and say was that Ariel had inherited John Paget's looks. Not wishing to draw attention to such an unwelcome fact, Molly squeezed Ariel's shoulder and said, "Go unpack your bag and leave your grandma to rest while I see what I can put together for dinner, honey, then we'll have a picnic up here. That okay with you, Mom?"

"Can't think of anything I'd like better." Hilda was tired, no question about it, and her breathing labored, but her smile shone out like a beacon in the fog. "Don't think I ever had a picnic in bed before. Don't think it was ever allowed when your father was alive. Guess maybe I've got more to look forward to than I thought, yesterday at this time."

How she made it out of the room and downstairs before she fell apart, Molly didn't know. Choking on emotion, she took refuge behind the antlered coatrack while she groped in her pocket for a tissue. But mopping her eyes did nothing to silence the accusations ringing in her head.

It's a bit late to shed tears now, Molly Paget. You were the only thing to stand between that poor woman in the bed upstairs and her bully of a husband, yet you walked out and left her to fend for herself when you knew she didn't have it in her to stand up to him. You're a pitiful excuse for a daughter and deserve every word of criticism and disapproval ever cast at you. How would you feel if Ariel grew up to abandon you the way you abandoned your mother?

Destroyed, that's how! Because Ariel was the most important person in the world to Molly.

But Hilda had had a husband, and what he thought and wanted and decreed had always carried the day, no matter how harsh or unreasonable his demands. If living with him had become too burdensome, all she'd had to do was pick up the phone. It wasn't as if Molly had disappeared without trace. From the day she left home, she'd kept in touch with her mother through letters. But those she received in return had been infrequent and stilted, as though her mother begrudged having to reply at all. The last had been sent eleven months ago and short enough that Molly could recall it almost word for word.

Dear Molly, Hilda had written. *Our winter has been hard. The kitchen pipes froze twice last week and the price of fish is very high. Cadie Boudelet's new grandchild came down with bronchitis, poor little thing. The Livingstons had a chimney fire last week and nearly burned the house down. Our TV broke and we have decided not to get another because there's never anything worth watching, so I try to get to the library once a week. I sold four quilts at Christmas which brought in a bit of extra money. It started snowing at the end of November and hasn't stopped since and here we are in April already. Your father hardly ever leaves the house because he's afraid of falling on the ice. Hoping this finds you and your little girl well, I remain your loving Mother.*

Typically there was no question about *their* life. No spark of interest in Ariel's doings and only the most cursory inquiry about her health. The apparent indifference had fueled a decade-long resentment in Molly which she'd been sure nothing could undo. But the unguarded joy on her mother's face when she realized who it was standing at her bedside left that resentment in tatters, and had Molly questioning her assessment of those sparse, uninformative letters.

Suddenly she saw the loneliness written between the lines; the utter emptiness of a woman who'd given up hope of the kind of affection which tied families together. The recognition left her awash in yet another wave of guilt.

"But, I'm here now, Momma," she whispered, stuffing the sodden tissues back in her pocket and fumbling her way down the darkened hall to the kitchen. "And I'll make up for the past by seeing to it that whatever future you've got left is the best I can make it."

Nothing in the kitchen had changed. The same old refrigerator, past its best when Molly had been a child, still clanked along in the corner. The same two-burner stove stood on the far side of the sink. What was surely the world's ugliest chrome kitchen set—table topped with gray Formica, chair seats padded with red plastic—filled what floor space was left. The only new addition was the calendar thumbtacked to the wall near the back door, and even it looked exactly like its predecessors, except for the date.

Small wonder her mother showed no interest in getting well. A caged hamster racing endlessly on its treadmill led a more interesting and varied existence.

There was canned tomato soup in the cupboard, and in the refrigerator a block of cheese, some butter, a jar of mayonnaise, and half a loaf of bread. Molly found the cast iron frying pan where it had always been, in the warming drawer below the oven, and set to work. She might have come a long way from the days when she'd worn hand-me-down clothes, but the lean years in between had taught her to make a nourishing meal out of whatever she happened to have on hand. Hot soup and grilled cheese sandwiches, with tea on the side, would serve for tonight.

The kettle was just coming to a boil and she was turning the sandwiches in the frying pan one last time when the back door shot open and sent a blast of cold air gusting around her ankles. But it didn't compare though to the chilly glare of the woman who came in with it.

Cadie Boudelet never had been one to smile much, but the drawstring of disapproval pulling at her mouth gave new definition to the term "grim-faced." "I heard you were back," she announced balefully. "Bad news travels fast in these parts."

"Lovely to see you again, too, Mrs. Boudelet," Molly said, unsurprised to find nothing had changed here, either. The Boudelets and every other neighbor had viewed her as an outcast ever since she turned ten—a Jezebel in the making, with the morals of an alley cat in heat already in evidence—and a warm welcome would have left her speechless. "Is there something I can do for you, or did you just stop by to be sociable and say hello?"

"Hah! Still got the same smart mouth you always had, I see." Cadie slammed an enameled casserole dish on the table and crossed her arms over her formidable breasts. "I brought your ma a bite for her supper, so you can throw out whatever you've got cooking there—unless you were making it for yourself, which is likely the case since you were never one to think of anybody's needs but your own."

Sorely tempted though she was to dump the contents of the casserole over the woman's self-righteous head, a brawl on her first night home would hardly further her mother's recovery, Molly decided. So steeling herself to restraint if not patience, she wiped her hands on the dish towel she'd tied around her waist and said, "I understand you've been very kind to my mother since she came home from the hospital, and for that I'm grateful. But now that I'm here, you need go to no more trouble on her behalf."

"No more trouble? Girl, a load of it walked in the door when you decided to set foot in town again, and all the fancy clothes and city airs in the world can't hide it. Just because you snagged yourself a rich husband don't change a thing and you'd have done your ma a bigger favor by staying away. She don't need the aggravation of your being here when she's got all she can do to deal with your daddy's passing.''

Just how unwisely Molly might have responded to that remark was forestalled by the sound of the front door opening and footsteps coming down the hall. A moment later, Dan Cordell appeared in the kitchen.

"Good grief!'' she exclaimed, exasperated. "Doesn't anyone around here believe in waiting to be invited before they march into someone else's house?''

"No need to,'' Cadie informed her. "People around here got nothing to hide—as a rule, that is. 'Course, that could change, depending on who's living in the house in question.''

Accurately sizing up the scene, Dan raised a placating hand. "Just thought I'd stop by to make sure you were handling things okay before I call it a day, Molly, that's all. Is that one of your fabulous casseroles I can smell, Cadie?''

The drawstring around her mouth relaxed enough to allow a smirk of pleasure to slip through. "It is. And there's plenty more at home, if you've got time to stop for a bite, Doctor.''

The smile he cast at the old biddy left Molly wondering how the icicles draped outside the window didn't melt on the spot. "Thanks, but it'll have to be some other time. I've got a dinner engagement tonight and I'm already running behind. Molly, can we speak privately a moment?''

"You listen to what the doctor tells you, girl,'' Cadie warned, wrapping her shawl around her head and yanking open the back door to let in another Arctic blast. "He knows what he's talking about and your ma's lucky he was there to look after her when she needed the best. He's a good man, is our Doctor Cordell.''

In the silence she left behind, Molly stared across the kitchen at Dan, an age-old bitterness souring her tongue. "Tell me something, Doctor. How come you're everybody's fair-haired darling despite your many past delinquencies, while I remain forever a pariah, no matter how much I might have reformed?''

"Maybe I work harder to change public opinion than you do, Molly," he said, propping up the wall with his altogether too impressive shoulders. "Or maybe I don't go quite as far out of my way to offend people. You've been home what…an hour? Two? And already you're squaring off with your next door neighbor. If I hadn't shown up when I did, you'd probably have wound up decking Cadie when you should be on your knees thanking her.''

It—*he!*—was the last straw! Cadie Boudelet was a tiresome, ignorant woman who seldom bothered to learn the facts before she arrived at a conclusion, which rendered her opinion of Molly, or anyone else for that matter, irrelevant. But that *he* should have the nerve to stand there mouthing holier-than-thou platitudes, as if the mere idea that Molly might not have achieved heights of perfection comparable to his caused him intolerable pain, just about made her throw up and she wasted no time telling him so.

"You make me sick to my stomach, Dan Cordell! If there's one thing I can't abide, it's a man who pretends he's above reproach to the one person in the world who knows differently. And if you think sticking 'Doctor' in front of your name entitles you to change history, you're even more arrogant than you are insufferable!''

CHAPTER TWO

"YOU don't think much of me, do you, Molly?" he said, glad she didn't have a kitchen knife at hand or he'd probably have been wearing it between his ribs.

"I don't think about you at all," she informed him loftily, "except when you force yourself to my notice. Then I find you irritating beyond words. So say whatever it is you came to say, then please leave."

He'd thought, when he heard she was coming back, that seeing her again wouldn't much affect him. Thought that age would have mellowed the fiery rebel he'd known briefly more years ago than he cared to count. She'd be a little plumper around the edges, both emotionally and physically; a little complacent and a lot less arrestingly gorgeous. Less inclined to fly off the handle, too. After all, she'd risen well above her impoverished beginnings, according to her mother, and had surely outgrown all those old resentments.

He'd been wrong on every count. The girl she'd been paled beside the woman she'd become. Spitting fury at him from across that sorry little kitchen, dark hair tumbling around her face, dark eyes flashing, her burgundy red skirt flinging an echoing slash of color across her magnificent cheekbones, she might have stepped out of a Russian drama, or a gypsy saga.

No wonder Cadie Boudelet had been on the verge of a stroke! Molly Paget had bloomed into much too exotic a specimen for the staid population of Harmony Cove to take in stride, and lost none of her rebelliousness in the process.

"If I'm irritating and insufferable, you're impossible," he said, fully aware that in firing a counterattack he left himself wide open to another verbal onslaught, but too intrigued by the challenge to let the opportunity pass. "I'm sorry if my being a doctor leaves you nauseated but the fact is, I earned the right to the title, just as you earned the right to call yourself a mother. And I fail to see what history has to do with the way things stand today."

"Not everyone's memory is as hazy as yours," she said, with a lot less passion than he'd expected. "Coming back here is like taking a one-way walk into the past. I'm hardly in the door before you're all lining up to tell me not to bother unpacking my bags."

"You storm back into town with both barrels blazing, ready to take on all comers, and wonder why no one's rushing to put out the welcome mat? It's not other people's perception of you that's the problem, Molly, it's that permanent chip on your shoulder."

"I'm not the one who put it there."

All at once, she looked defenseless, leaving him to wonder if she was quite as hard-boiled as she liked to appear. Her mouth drooped and if it weren't that she'd always known how to use those stunning eyes to good effect, he might have been fooled into thinking they held the faint sheen of tears.

As if anyone or anything could make Molly Paget cry!

Shoving aside the preposterous urge to take her in his arms, he shifted his weight so that both feet were planted firmly on the floor, and rammed his hands in his jacket pockets, out of temptation's way. "You *are* the one who chooses to keep carrying it around, though. Take a little well-meant advice from an old friend, Molly: drop the attitude and learn to give a little, and I'll bet you dollars to doughnuts you won't have to take nearly as much flak as you seem to expect.''

''And it was for this that you wanted to speak privately with me? To dish out—?''

''No. Consider it a bonus thrown in without charge. The reason I dropped by is that I just got word the public health nurse is held up at one of the outlying farms and probably won't make it back in time to look in on your mother. Hilda needs two different medications before she goes to sleep. If you like, I can walk you through what they entail or, if you're not comfortable with that, I'll come back again last thing and administer them myself.''

Her face told him she didn't much like either option. ''It depends what you mean by medication. If it involves sticking needles in her—''

''It doesn't,'' he said, unable to curb a smile. ''If it did, there'd be no question but that I'd be the one to do the sticking, if for no other reason than I remember you don't cope well with needles.''

''You do?'' Her mouth formed a perfect O of surprise, reminding him of a rosebud about to unfurl.

''Uh-huh.'' He wrenched his gaze away, and stared at the calendar on the wall, which he found a whole lot less distracting than her face. ''You cut yourself on a glass, your first day waitressing at The Ivy Tree. I drove you to my father's office and when he told you you'd need stitches, you just about passed out.''

She turned her left hand palm up and stroked her right forefinger over the faded scar. Her clothes were expensive. Her gold hoop earrings and the bangle around her wrist held the subtle gleam of the real twenty-four carat stuff. Yet she wore no rings, he noticed. No diamond solitaire or wedding band to proclaim her marital status.

"I'm surprised you remember that," she murmured.

So was he. He hadn't thought of the incident in years, but having found a crack in his defenses, nostalgia streamed through him like warm honey. She'd been irresistible as sun-kissed peaches, the summer they'd met. Sweet, delectable, and ripe for the picking, even with blood dripping down her uniform, and he'd wasted no time volunteering to be her driver. "There are a lot of things I remember about that summer, Molly," he said.

Her face grew shuttered. "There are a lot I'd prefer to forget. I was very young at the time."

"Yes. A lot younger than you led me to believe."

"And you," she said, "were a great deal more callous than was necessary. Telling me you'd grown tired of me was enough to get yourself off the hook. There was no need to parade my replacement under my nose to prove the point. No need to humiliate me in front of the other waitresses by letting your new girlfriend order me around as if I were her personal servant."

"Either memory serves me badly, or you're confusing me with someone else. I recall no such thing."

"Her name," she said, spitting out the words as if they were bullets, "was Francine. And she wrapped her legs so far around your waist when she rode pillion on your motorcycle that she looked like a boa constrictor preparing to devour her next meal."

How he didn't choke on his laughter was a direct contradiction of everything he'd learned in medical school. He should have needed resuscitating! "You always had such a way with words, Molly. It's nice to see you haven't lost your touch."

But she wasn't amused. If anything, the way she skewered him in a glare left him suspecting she'd been hurt more by his rejection than she let on at the time.

What she couldn't begin to guess was that he hadn't exactly walked away heart-whole, either. But even he'd had to draw the line when he'd learned she was only seventeen and not the almost-twenty she'd claimed. He might not have amounted to much in those days, but nor had he been completely without conscience.

"I'm sorry if I was less than sensitive."

"I'm not," she said bluntly. "If anything, I'm grateful you showed yourself in your true colors. You gave me the incentive to make a fresh start somewhere else."

"How so?"

She started to reply, then seemed to think better of it. The flush on her cheeks deepened and she turned to the stove, leaving him to stare at her back. "Never mind. Let's just say I grew up in a hurry and realized I'd been miles out of my depth in thinking we could ever have lasted as a couple."

"So you left town, met the man of your dreams, settled down and started a family."

She tilted her shoulder in a small shrug. "I met the man of my dreams. Did you ever meet the woman of yours?"

"I'm not married yet, if that's what you're asking."

"Why not? Haven't found anyone with good enough bloodlines to assume the role?"

"It so happens that I have," he said, ignoring the taunt. "Which reminds me, I'm running late and keeping her waiting, as usual." He tore a blank sheet from the prescription pad in his pocket and scribbled directions on it. "Here's what your mother will need before you settle her for the night. The meds are on a tray, on the dresser in her room. If you run into any difficulties or have any concerns at all, call my service and they'll page me. And don't forget to make that appointment to see me tomorrow at the clinic.''

"If I have time." She tossed the answer over her shoulder with calculated defiance.

"Make the time, Molly," he warned her. "This isn't a request, it's an order, and if you care about your mother at all, you'll follow it."

He kept her cooling her heels over half an hour when she showed up as scheduled, at eleven-thirty the next morning. Though tempted to cancel the appointment with a curt "My time's valuable, too!" when told he'd been called to the hospital, she thought better of it and took a seat in the waiting area.

Meeting him on neutral ground, especially one as sterile as the setting where he shared space with two other doctors, was infinitely preferable to having him drop by the house whenever the mood took him. The less personal their contact, and the less he saw of Ariel, the better.

The shock of meeting him again, of finding him in charge of her mother's case, was still too new. Molly felt brittle as blown glass around him—completely at the mercy of emotions as untoward as they were unanticipated.

Such a state of fragility was dangerous. It left her susceptible to letting slip little details which could lead to his asking questions about Ariel's father which she wasn't prepared to answer. But avoiding him was impossible, so deal with him she must. Now that she'd had time to digest her mother's situation, she had questions of her own— concerns which hadn't immediately occurred to her when he'd made his house call yesterday, but which definitely needed to be addressed.

As well, there was the issue of the fantasy life her

mother had dreamed up on her behalf and which Molly felt compelled to tone down with at least a smidgen of truth, for Ariel's sake if no one else's.

"Well, I had to tell people something!" Hilda had protested, when Molly had confronted her on the subject of the phantom rich husband waiting in the wings. "It was the only way to shut people up. Even though no one knew for sure the real reason you left town, it didn't stop the gossip."

"But, Mom, what if someone asks Ariel about her supposed daddy—why he didn't come with us, or what sort of work he does or why her last name's Paget and not Smith or Brown or Jones?"

"Why would anyone question a child her age about things like that?"

"Your nosy neighbors—the very first chance they get, and we both know it!" Molly had shaken her head in dismay. "If you felt you had to lie, couldn't you just have kept it simple and said I'd taken a job somewhere else? Or better yet, let them have their say and ignore them?"

"No," her mother had said, with more vigor than Molly would have believed possible two hours before. "Why, Alice Livingston heard you were in jail, if you can imagine! So I put a stop to things the only way I knew how and that was to spread news they didn't want to hear. Once word got out you'd married a rich man, you became boring and people found something else to wag tongues over."

"I'm surprised anyone believed you in the first place!"

Hilda's face had broken into a smile, and she'd covered Molly's hand with hers. "Child, even your father believed me, and I never said a word to make him think differently! I know you despise me for letting him treat you the way he did, so you might find this hard to understand, but it hurt me, Molly, to have to stand back and do nothing when he went after you. It hurt me as much as it hurt you. The only difference was, my bruises didn't show.''

Exhausted from the long day's travel, Ariel was already asleep in the little room down the hall. The house was peaceful, the curtains drawn against the bitter night, and nothing but the low drone of the furnace in the cellar to compete with the budding intimacy between the two women. As far as Molly could recall, it was the first time she and her mother had ever exchanged confidences so freely. It allowed her to ask a question she'd never dared voice before.

''Then why didn't you leave him, Mom? Why didn't you take me and just run away? How could you stay married to such a brute?''

Looking haggard suddenly, her mother had wilted against the pillows. ''You said it yourself more than once, Molly. We live in a backwater here, about a hundred years behind the outside world. I was forty-three when I had you, and women of my generation didn't walk out on their husbands, it's as simple as that. And he wasn't always bad. When we were first married, he was a lovely man. But the accident changed him. Losing his leg cost him his livelihood, child. He'd always been big and strong. Able to do anything. But a cripple's no use on a fishing boat when the weather's stirring up a storm, and it killed something in him to know he wasn't the leader of the fleet anymore.''

''Having only one leg didn't hamper him too much when he was chasing me down the street in a blind rage.''

''Because you reminded him too much of how he used to be—healthy and strong and independent. He was eaten up with anger, Molly, and it made him do and say wicked things at times.''

"At times? There was hardly a day went by that he didn't make me miserable! If I was wild, he did his part in driving me to it."

Her mother had sighed and squeezed her hand again. "Don't let yourself fall into that trap," she said sagely. "He passed on his looks to you, and you're beautiful for it, but don't take on his bitterness and make it your own. It'll sour the rest of your life, if you do, and come to infect that sweet granddaughter of mine, as well."

Molly had had all night to mull over her mother's words and much though it galled her to admit it, they made a certain sort of sense. Coming back to Harmony Cove had made her realize the extent to which John Paget still warped her thinking from beyond the grave. But only because she allowed him to. Although breaking the habit wouldn't be easy, it was the only way she'd ever free herself from his painful influence.

The clinic's outer door flew open and Dan strode in, bringing a cold, fresh whiff of snow and frigid sea air with him. "Hi, Molly," he said, breezing past and stopping at the receptionist's desk to pick up his messages. "Have a seat in my office and I'll be with you in a sec."

But it was closer to ten minutes before he followed. "Cripes," he said, flinging himself into the beaten-up old chair behind the equally battered desk, "what a morning!"

"Actually, it's now the afternoon," Molly said, glancing pointedly at the clock on the wall. "And my appointment was for eleven-thirty."

"Sorry about that," he said, sounding anything but.

"You could have fooled me!"

He fixed her in the sort of semi-stern, semi-cajoling gaze which no doubt left most of his patients, especially the women, slobbering with delight and falling all over themselves to do his bidding. The way the laugh lines deepened at the corners of his eyes and his lashes drooped over those brilliant blue irises struck Molly as nothing less than ludicrous. Did he think he was auditioning for leading man in a soap opera or something?

"Babies don't always show up when they're supposed to, Molly, you should know that," he said. "Or was your daughter the rare exception and born exactly on schedule?"

When Ariel was born wasn't something she was willing to discuss with him but it was clear from the way he continued to regard her that he expected a reply. There was a layer of hidden steel under all that warm, fuzzy charm. "Not quite," she said.

"There you are, then!" He flashed one of his thousand megawatt grins and slapped the flat of his hand against the even flatter planes of his stomach. "Are you hungry?"

"I beg your pardon?"

"I said, are you—?"

"I heard what you said. I'm just not sure I understand the reason you said it, Doctor."

He rolled his eyes, another in his repertoire of disarming mannerisms. "Will you for Pete's sake give over with the 'Doctor' business and stop acting as if you just swallowed a lemon? I'm offering to buy you lunch, not cut out your heart."

It was on the tip of her tongue to tell him he'd done the latter eleven years before without benefit of medical expertise, but his ego was inflated enough. "Thank you, but no. Ariel's sitting with my mother and I don't want to leave her alone any longer than I have to."

"You can spare another half hour," he said. "It's going to take that long to sort out what we're going to do about your mom anyway, and I'm talking about a quick sandwich somewhere, not a seven-course dinner at Le Caveau.''

As if a man of his fine lineage would ever take a woman from Wharf Street to Le Caveau! The most exclusive restaurant for miles around didn't even *hire* people from there, let alone welcome them as guests.

He scooped the phone across the desk toward her. ''If you're worried about Ariel and Hilda, give Alice Livingston a call and ask her to keep an eye on them. She stops in every day around this time anyway with a bowl of soup or something for your mom.''

''I'd rather have my teeth pulled!''

He treated her to another grin. ''Don't tell me you've already locked horns with her, as well!''

''We've yet to come face-to-face since I got back, but it's a foregone conclusion that when we do, it won't be a happy reunion. And she won't be dropping off soup or anything else, come to that. I left Ariel with strict instructions not to open the door to anyone.''

''So she and Hilda are waiting for you to go home and make lunch?''

He'd handed her the perfect opening to decline his invitation, but what was the point of lying when this meeting had to take place sooner, rather than later? ''No. I left sandwiches and milk in case I was delayed getting back. Ariel will make sure neither she nor my mother starves.''

''Isn't that child a bit young to left with so much responsibility?''

''She's ten—''

''Ten?'' He raised his eyebrows questioningly. ''That must mean she—''

''T…ten times more capable than girls nearly twice her age.'' Shaking inside, Molly tacked on the qualifier, aghast at how close she'd come to endangering the one secret she was most committed to protect. Oh, the pitfalls of deceit! "And I always keep my cell phone turned on when I'm not home, so she knows she can get in touch any time."

"You make it sound as if you leave her alone often."

"No, I don't! Not that it's any of your business, but if she needs to call me from school or a friend's house or something, and I happen to be out..." She trailed into silence, aware that she sounded far too defensive for a woman supposedly confident of her parenting skills.

As if he'd noticed the same thing, he regarded her thoughtfully a moment and she tensed, waiting for another probing observation. But in the end, he merely rose out of the chair and said, "In that case, there's no reason at all we can't have lunch while we talk about your mom's case, is there?"

There's every reason in the world! she thought. *Time spent with you is like walking a tightrope and knowing there's no safety net waiting to catch me if I trip and fall!*

And trip she surely would, unless she wrestled her runaway emotions under control. But he seemed determined to thwart her at every turn. "Watch your step," he ordered, taking her arm as they approached the intersection of Fundy Street, Harmony Cove's main road. "It's slippery underfoot and you won't be much use to your mom if you slip and break an ankle."

She wore enough clothes to keep out the cold but not, it seemed, enough to stop the warmth from his hand creeping through the layers of her sweater and coat. Or was it just proximity to the only man who'd ever touched her deepest passions that sent awareness flushing over her skin like the kiss of the summer sun?

"I'm quite capable of crossing the street unaided," she said.

"Not in those boots you're not," he informed her cheerfully. "You need to get yourself something a bit more serviceable if you're going to be here more than a day or two. How long are you planning to stick around, by the way?"

"As long as my mother needs me, of course."

"That could mean indefinitely, Molly. Are you really prepared to make that kind of sacrifice?"

"Yes," she said, too focused on the fact that he hadn't let go of her arm, even though they were now safely across the road and walking on bare, dry pavement again, to notice the trap he'd set.

He noticed, though, and didn't pass up the chance to shove her face-first into it. "But what about your husband, my dear? If you were my wife, I can't say I'd be too thrilled at being left to fend for myself while you travel to the other end of the country to play nursemaid to the mother-in-law I've never met."

"That's one reason you're not my husband," she said, congratulating herself on having sidestepped his question rather neatly. "You didn't measure up to my expectations."

"And the other reason of course being that I didn't volunteer for the job." As if he hadn't rattled her nerves to breaking point already, he added injury to insult by marching her down a side lane and strong-arming her through the door to the one place guaranteed to unravel her completely. "In you go, sweet thing. The waitresses aren't as fetching as some I used to know, but The Ivy Tree still makes the best club sandwiches in town."

It was like being thrust on stage to reprise a role she hadn't played in years. Everything was familiar, except the script. Panic closing in on her thicker than an Atlantic fog in November, she swung around, bent only on escape, and came smack up against the unyielding wall of his chest with such force that she almost fell.

Clawing blindly at his jacket, she struggled to maintain her balance along with her composure. Would have given ten years off her life to toss out some flippant remark that might fool him into believing this particular café was no different from any other. And could manage nothing more than a breathless, ''Oops! I caught my heel in the welcome mat.''

''I told you those boots were useless,'' he said.

Not entirely! Aimed in a kick at the right place, they could do substantial damage to a man, and the smug grin which accompanied his latest remark left Dan Cordell in grave danger of discovering that fact for himself.

Unaware of how close he'd come to limiting his potential for producing future heirs, he caught the attention of the hostess and inveigled her into seating them at a fireside table ahead of two other couples who'd been eyeing it. Molly supposed she should be grateful he hadn't wanted the booth by the window to which she'd been assigned when she worked there.

''Club sandwiches and coffee for two,'' he told the middle-aged waitress who waddled over to take their order.

''Make mine a spinach salad,'' Molly said, determined to assert her independence before her entire life spun so far beyond her control she'd never be able to rein it in again, ''with tea.''

''Sugar and cream?'' the waitress inquired, scribbling on her pad.

''Just lemon, please.''

''The works for me, Charlene,'' Dan said. ''I need all the sweetening I can get.''

Charlene, who had to be all of fifty if she was a day,

giggled like a schoolgirl and slapped his arm playfully. "Oh, Doctor!"

"How do you do it?" Molly asked him, when they were alone again.

He glanced up from contemplating his short, immaculately clean nails. "Do what?" he said, all blue-eyed innocence.

Innocent as a wolf on the prowl!

"As if you don't know," she scoffed. "That woman's well past the age where she's taken in by a smooth-talker, but one look from you and she just about fell out of her uniform!"

"Did she?" he said, reaching across the table to toy briefly with her fingers. "I can't say I noticed. I'm too caught up remembering how you looked wearing yours, way back when."

"Slightly indecent, probably," she said, snatching her hand away. "As I recall, the tunic skirt was very short."

"I recall your long, gorgeous legs. And how you came close to smacking me in the mouth for commenting on them."

She only remembered his mouth and how it had driven her wild when he'd made love to her. "Never mind all that," she said, sounding as starched as the lace curtains hanging at the café windows. "We're here to talk about my mother. Right now, she's spending all day in bed because she can't manage the stairs. If I were to eliminate that problem, what kind of options would she have for getting around?"

"When she's ready for it, primarily by using a wheelchair. I've already mentioned the possibility, but there's so little space to maneuver in her bedroom and, as you say, the stairs make it difficult for her to be brought down to the main floor, so there hasn't been much point in pursuing the idea. Frankly she'd have been better off recuperating in a nursing home but she flat-out refused to entertain the idea.''

''If I were to make different living arrangements—something that would permit her more mobility—would she still require daily visits from the nurse?''

''No,'' he said. ''In fact, freeing her from that bed would do more to speed her progress than just about anything we can offer in the way of medical care. Of course, she'll need ongoing drug therapy to combat her asthma and osteoporosis, and probably something for pain management for at least another few weeks, but it's my guess her present living conditions are the main reason she's making such a slow recovery. Shut-aways don't have a whole lot to motivate them to get well, Molly.''

''Especially not when they're abandoned by their only living relative, right?''

''It surely doesn't help.'' He shot her a level look across the table. ''Sorry if that hurts, but it's the truth.''

She sat back as their meal arrived, but as soon as they were alone again, said, ''Not that I feel I owe you or anyone else an explanation, but if I'd heard about the accident when it happened, instead of over a month after the fact, I'd have been here a lot sooner.''

''Hilda wouldn't hear of it.''

''I'm her next of kin. You had an obligation to let me know.''

''My first obligation was to my patient. As it is, I went against her wishes in allowing social services to contact you.'' He fixed her in another glance. ''For what it's worth, I'm glad I did.''

Uncertain how to interpret his last remark, she poked at the limp spinach salad in front of her and wished she'd ordered the club sandwich instead. "Will she still need to see you?"

"Occasionally, once she's past the present stage of recovery. But don't try to initiate too many changes too soon. Let's see how she does over the next while, first. If she makes significant progress, the visits can be cut to once a week, then less often as she continues to improve."

"If I were to drive her there, could she come to the clinic, instead of you having to come to the house?"

"Sure, if you can manage to get her there in one piece."

"I'm not planning to trundle her down the hill in a wheelchair and risk tipping her into the gutter, if that's what you're implying! I'll trade in my rental car for a minivan. I'm no doctor, but getting her out of that house, even if it's only to come for a checkup, has to be a benefit."

"I agree. But give her a few more days in bed first."

"I heard you the first time, Dan. And even if I hadn't, I'm not so blind that I can't see she's got a long recovery ahead of her."

He shrugged. "Fine. Any more questions?"

"Not at the moment."

"Then perhaps you'll answer a couple for me."

"Of course." She dabbed at her mouth with her napkin and stared him squarely in the eye. "Fire away."

"You haven't said a word about your father. Why not?"

"Because I don't care about him. I'd even go so far as to say I'm glad he's dead. I'd have held my nose and attended his funeral if I'd known about it, but only because it would have made it easier for my mother to have me there."

He blew out a breath. "You don't believe in pulling your punches, do you?"

"I don't believe in lying to save face."

"In that case, you won't mind telling me this: Why, if you're married, do you still go by the name Paget, and why aren't you wearing a wedding ring, Molly?"

CHAPTER THREE

"THAT'S two questions," Molly said, amazed that she managed to sound perfectly sane when she was near to suffocating with panic. "Which one should I answer?"

"Both," he said inexorably.

"It's easier to get rid of a husband than it is to face the world without one," had been her mother's rationale the night before. "If people ask, you can always say he died or something. At least you won't be condemned for being a widow."

"In this town, I just might be!" Molly had said ruefully. "They're likely to think I murdered him for his supposed fortune."

"Well, if you're going to have an imaginary husband, he might as well have money. Dream big, I always say. If folks are determined to gossip—and let's face it, it's what makes the world go round in these parts—give them something they can really sink their teeth into. And Molly Paget coming back to town respectable and rich is about as juicy a tidbit as they've chewed on in years."

She'd laughed at that. They both had, the shared conspiracy forging another long overdue bonding between mother and daughter. But it didn't seem so funny or clever now, with Dan scrutinizing her, feature by feature.

Mind racing, Molly tried to decide between presenting herself as a widow or a divorcée. Widowhood might promote a more sympathetic response, but it was also likely to invite further questions, especially from a doctor.

Divorce, on the other hand, was common enough that it rarely aroused much interest.

She gave a tiny shrug, as much to disguise the fact that she was shaking like a leaf, as for theatrical effect, and settled for a lie of omission over outright deceit. "I'd have thought it was obvious. I don't wear a ring and I go by my maiden name because marriage didn't work out for me. I've been a single parent for years."

"I see."

She was afraid he did—far more than she ever intended he should. Subterfuge had never been her strong point and the flimsy evasions she'd handed out wouldn't fool a half-wit, let alone a man of his intelligence.

"You have sole custody of your daughter, then?"

"Yes. Why do you sound so surprised?"

"Because it's unusual in this day and age. Most courts award joint guardianship of minor children."

"Only if it's something both parents want."

And you didn't, Dan Cordell!

"Let's face it, sweet Molly," he'd said, that hot August evening he ended their affair by trying to make it sound like a mutual decision, "it's as well we're calling it quits now because we wouldn't have lasted much longer anyway. Next month I'm off to Europe for a year, maybe two. Even if I weren't, I'm not ready to settle down and you…" He'd sighed and tried to look properly pained, as though to say, *This is hurting me more than it's hurting you,* which was a laugh and a half! "You're only seventeen. Much too young to be thinking about anything long-term, especially with a guy who still hasn't figured out what he wants to do with his life."

The new and reformed Daniel Cordell, M.D., swung his head in bewilderment. "I don't understand how any man could turn away from his child. I've probably delivered close to a hundred babies over the last few years, and each one's as big a thrill as the first. I don't mind telling you, being there to watch my firstborn come into the world is something I look forward to with the utmost pleasure.''

''You talk as if it's a fait accompli that you'll father a child.''

He laughed. ''It's not a done deal, if that's what you mean. I'm conventional enough to believe marriage comes before children.''

These days, maybe! But where were your fine scruples when you seduced me and forgot to use a condom?

''Are you planning to get married soon?'' It shouldn't hurt so much to ask, but it did. Pain shot through her like a live wire, leaving her winded from the shock of it.

''We're in no hurry. We're both busy with our careers. It'll happen when the time's right. What about you? Ever think of remarrying?''

''No,'' she said. ''I'm too busy raising a daughter and running a business—and now, looking after my mother. I don't need the complication of a husband.''

He dropped two lumps of sugar in his coffee, added a dollop of cream and stirred thoughtfully. ''But you must have been glad of one when you were pregnant, and especially when you gave birth?''

Straightforward enough, at least on the surface, the question slipped between the cracks in her defenses, and laid open a wound too grievous to endure a second time.

In the blink of an eye, it all came back. The fear, even though there'd been three nurses and two doctors in attendance—kind, competent professionals every one. The pain which nothing could assuage. The terrible, aching loneliness, even though Rob had been there the whole time, cheering her on.

But Molly had wanted Dan. Wanted *him* to wipe the sweat from her forehead. Wanted his hand to clutch when the contractions grew too strong to bear, and his encouragement when exhaustion wore her down to tears. And most of all wanted him to hold her in his arms and kiss her and tell her she was brave and wonderful and that he loved her, when at last it was all over and Ariel lay, bathed and sweetly sleeping, in her bassinet.

"Why so downcast? Don't tell me you went through that time alone, Molly!"

She blinked and wrenched herself back to the present, taking comfort in the tangible warmth of the log fire smoldering in the hearth, and the pots of silk ivy trailing from brass planters hanging on the wall. "No," she said softly, the break in her voice caused by another, more recent sorrow. "Rob was by my side the entire time, and he was wonderful."

"At least you have some good memories then."

More than he could begin to know but almost certainly not the kind he imagined. She doubted Dan could appreciate or understand the relationship she'd shared with Rob. Most men wouldn't.

"I really have to go," she said, pushing away from the table not just because the afternoon was slipping away but because it was safer to put an end to a conversation which had trespassed into territory altogether too personal. "Ariel and my mother have been alone long enough."

He was out of his chair in a flash and helping her with her coat despite her protests that she could manage on her own. She didn't want the scent of his cologne drifting out to touch her, or his fingers brushing warmly over the nape of her neck, or his breath ruffling her hair. She wanted him at least six feet away, in a starched white medical jacket and smelling of antiseptic.

"I'll walk you out," he said.

"No need. I know the way."

"I'm sure!" He pulled a credit card from an inside pocket and made for the cashier's desk. "I'll walk you out anyway, as soon as I've settled up what we owe."

Not about to waste opportunity when it stared her in the face, she headed for the door and almost made it out of the square and onto the main street before he caught up with her. "If I didn't know better, I'd think you're afraid to be seen with me, Molly," he chided genially.

"I'd think you'd have better things to do than idle away the afternoon with someone who isn't even a patient."

If she hadn't been so occupied trying to dislodge the hand he persisted in clamping around her elbow, she might have noticed sooner the woman headed toward them, and had the presence of mind to cross the road before the almighty Mrs. Daniel Cordell Senior descended like a crow about to feast on a hapless quarry.

Frozen-faced, she brought her glance to rest on Molly. "What a surprise, Daniel," she remarked, her cultured tones ringing with disdain. "I expected you to be spending the afternoon gainfully employed in caring for the sick and down-at-heel."

"Nice to run into you, too, Yvonne," he said. "You remember Molly Paget, don't you?"

"I don't believe we've ever met, though the name's vaguely familiar." The hint of a frown ruffled the smooth perfection of her brow. "Wasn't it a Paget who drove his car directly into the path of a train, thereby managing to kill himself and leave his widow crippled for life?"

"More or less," Dan said with undisguised annoyance. "But leave it you to paraphrase the incident so succinctly. Pity your memory's not quite as acute in this instance.

You met Molly long before her parents suffered such a tragedy. Over ten years ago, in fact.''

"Did I? I can't imagine how or why.''

"I brought her to the house for dinner once.''

"Ah yes, now that you mention it, I do seem to recall some such incident.'' She might as well have said, *Wasn't she the girl who didn't know the difference between a wineglass and a demitasse? Dear heaven, Daniel, have you lost your mind?* "And you're still friends?''

"Hardly!'' Bristling, Molly at last succeeded in prying her elbow free. "Dr. Cordell was merely bringing me up to speed on my mother's prognosis.''

"Very commendable of him I'm sure, darling, but wouldn't that dreadful clinic he's so attached to have been a more appropriate place to request a consultation?''

Funny how a tone of voice sometimes said more than the words themselves. Coming out of Yvonne Cordell's mouth, "darling" was almost a profanity.

Dan didn't come right out and say he was of the same opinion, but if anyone had ever looked at Molly the way he looked at his mother then, she'd have withered on the spot. "Keep me posted on your plans, Molly,'' he said, tilting his shoulder in such a way that Mrs. Cordell was totally excluded from the exchange. "And please call me before you decide on any drastic changes. I want to be sure your mom can handle whatever it is you've got in mind.''

"Of course. Thank you for lunch.''

"My pleasure.'' He caught her gloved hand and gave it a lingering squeeze. "Maybe we can do it again at a more leisurely pace.''

A lovely idea even if it was quite out of the question! But telling herself so didn't stop her heart from leaping into overdrive and running amok. Glad he couldn't see the upheaval he'd caused, she said, "I doubt I'll be able to spare the time—or you, either, come to that, busy doctor that you are."

His smile flowed over her, warm and disgracefully beguiling. "Sure we will. Even I take a day off once in a while and we've got a lot of catching up to do."

Behind him, Yvonne Cordell let a sigh gust forth. It hung in the air, a visible cloud of exasperation and disbelief, as cold as the woman who'd ejected it. She might just as well have come right out and snorted, *Lunch again? With this little vixen? Over my dead body!*

Mind whirling, Dan watched as she took off down the street, her long legs eating up the distance with ease despite her high-heeled boots. Graceful, elegant and reeking of success, she'd have been an intimidating presence if it weren't for her eyes. *They* told another story, one fraught with a wariness which bordered on fear. And therein lay the mystery, because the one thing the old Molly Paget had never shown was a speck of fear, no matter how harshly life treated her.

Her father could have beaten her black and blue, the neighbors spat on her and the town forefathers tried to burn her at the stake for her supposed sins, and she'd have defied the lot of them rather than cave in and beg for leniency. She'd have stood tall and proud, looking for all the world like some pagan princess, with her hair flying around her shoulders in black disarray and her eyes flashing, and told the lot of them that if heaven was filled with types like them, she'd prefer to roast in hell! And at their collective gasp of outrage, she'd have laughed.

So what had brought about the change in her?

A number of possible reasons came to mind, all of them disturbing. In a professional capacity, he'd seen his share of victimized women—creatures so timid and down-trodden that they'd come to believe they deserved the abuse directed at them.

Was Molly one of them but able, by virtue of money, to hide behind a veneer of success?

He didn't know. But he intended to find out.

"...quite inexcusable, Daniel!"

Molly had climbed into a burgundy Taurus. Waiting for a gap in the flow of traffic, she pulled out from the curb, made an illegal U-turn, and shot back along Fundy Street toward the harbor. He might just as well have been another iron lamppost with dirty snow piled around its base, for all the notice she took of him as she zoomed past.

"And for someone like that!"

"Hmm?" Aware that his mother had been rattling on for the last several minutes, he glanced up absently, wondering when Molly had decided to get her glorious hair cut so short. Not that the chic new styling didn't suit her. On the contrary, it fit her present image perfectly.

"I'm talking about your fiancée," Yvonne snapped. "How do you suppose she'd have felt if *she'd* been the one to come across you arming that woman out of a coffee shop after you'd had your receptionist phone to cancel your lunch date with Summer at Pierre's?"

"I couldn't spare the time for lunch at Pierre's with Summer."

"But you found the time for Ms. Paget?"

"I *made* the time, Yvonne. There's a difference."

His mother treated him to the kind of long-suffering look which, before his retirement, she'd directed at his father whenever he'd excused himself from a social function to answer the needs of a patient. "Clearly you did. Well, it's my birthday two weeks from this Sunday, and your father's organizing a small dinner party at The Harmony Cove Inn for dinner. Dare I ask if you'll *make* the time to join us?''

"I'll be there," he said. "Gerry Clarke owes me a Sunday off. Barring some unforeseen catastrophe, I don't anticipate being needed at the hospital.''

"And how often have I heard *that* before?''

"Many times, I don't doubt. But you can't have it both ways, Yvonne. You were the one bursting with maternal pride when I finally got my act together and decided to follow in Dad's footsteps, so it's no use moaning now about the obligations that come with the job.''

"The 'job,' Daniel, never had to involve buying into a seedy clinic practice on the wrong side of town. Even your father never went to those extremes to prove his dedication to his profession.''

"I guess not," he said vaguely, eyes still trained on the burgundy Taurus as it hung a left and swerved into the parking lot of a strip mall at the end of the road.

His mother let out a hiss, a sure sign she was winding up for another lecture on her favorite subject. "To find real satisfaction in his life, a man has to achieve balance, Daniel, and I fear it's sadly lacking in yours. Summer's a tolerant woman and will make an ideal doctor's wife should you ever get around to setting a wedding date, but I caution you against taking her for granted. Just because she puts up a good front and hides disappointment well doesn't mean she's not every bit as vulnerable to hurt as the rest of us. I can only pray word doesn't get back to her that you were seen arming another woman through the middle of town.''

The advice sloughed off him like rain sheeting down a pane of glass. Summer, aristocratic and coolly beautiful, surveyed the world with the supreme confidence of one born to privilege. Insecurity was as foreign a concept to her as he'd once thought fear was to Molly.

Which brought him back full circle to the question still gnawing at the back of his mind: who or what was creating the anxiety clouding the lovely Ms. Paget's gorgeous brown eyes?

Judging by the speed with which she came barreling out of her front door, Cadie Boudelet must have been lurking at her living-room window specifically to accost Molly the second she stepped out of the car.

"Shameful, that's what it is!" she brayed, scuttling down her front walkway. "Hours you've been gone, that I know for a fact because I saw you leave, so I come to your mother's house to make sure the poor soul's being properly looked after, and what do I find but the door locked in my face for the first time in years and that child of yours mouthing off at me through the mail slot, telling me I'm not needed."

"Good. She was following my instructions. If you've got a problem with that, take it up with me and leave my daughter out of it," Molly said.

"Everyone on Wharf Street has a problem with you, girl. Do you think showing up here at the eleventh hour in your fancy clothes and your fancy car changes who you really are underneath?"

"Perish the thought!" Dismissing her, Molly popped open the trunk of the car and hauled out a wheelchair.

"And what," Cadie demanded, eyeing the thing as if it were the devil's own handiwork, "do you propose doing with that contraption?"

"Isn't it obvious? Strap my mother in it, shove her down the hill and hope somebody catches her before she rolls off the end of the dock."

Leaving the old bat to chew on that, Molly loaded the few things she'd picked up at the supermarket into the chair and wheeled it up to the house.

Ariel met her at the door, all smiles. "You didn't have to hurry back, Mommy. Like I told you when you phoned, me and Grandma were okay without you."

"'Grandma and I,' sweetheart," she said automatically, "and that's good to know. Were you bored?"

"No, we had the best time! After lunch, we played checkers, and I brushed Grandma's hair and she told me stories about when you were growing up."

A heavily edited version, Molly was sure. "Sounds wonderful. Let me run up and let her know I'm home, then we'll have tea and cake."

"She's sleeping right now. That's why I came downstairs. I was going to wash the dishes and surprise you, but then you got here before I could do it. Mommy, do you know what?"

Aglow with excitement, she hopped from one foot to the other and Molly couldn't help but wonder if there'd ever been a time, when she herself was a child, that her smile had lit up that dim hallway with such radiance. Had she ever known such unfettered happiness, such certainty that nothing could go awry with her world?

"What, sweetheart?"

"I'm going to be a nurse and look after sick people when I grow up. Grandma says I have magic healing hands."

So Ariel took after Dan in at least one respect, after all! Pressing a kiss to the satin soft skin of her daughter's cheek, Molly said thickly, "You're magic through and through, honey. I thought you already knew that."

Daylight had faded by the time Hilda woke up from her nap. "Molly, you didn't really say that!" she exclaimed between gasps of laughter, when she heard of the episode with Cadie Boudelet.

"Certainly I did. She was itching to attribute another failing to my already vast repertoire, and you wouldn't have wanted me to disappoint her, would you?"

"She'll be organizing a lynch mob before you know it."

"Or burning me in effigy. Quit wheezing, Mom, it's not good for you."

"Oh, but it is because it's true what they say. Laughter *is* the best medicine." Brighter-eyed than Molly would've thought possible the day before, her mother shuffled toward the edge of the bed. "Well, did you bring up that chair for decoration, or are we going for a spin?"

"Those stairs are just as deadly as the hill outside, you know. Sure you trust me?"

Molly spoke with a smile but her mother's face turned solemn when she replied, "With my very life, child. You're here, aren't you, taking on the whole neighborhood to be a good daughter to a woman who hasn't earned the right to ask it of you?"

"Let all that go, Mom. It's in the past." Scooping an arm around her shoulders, Molly pulled her mother into a gentle hug before inching her toward the edge of the bed. "Let's just concentrate instead on today and getting you mobile."

It shouldn't have been difficult. Hilda was a featherweight and with Ariel there to help, Molly hadn't anticipated a problem. But there was barely room to accommodate a stool beside the bed, let alone anything as cumbersome as a wheelchair, and she knew from her mother's stifled moan and the pinched pallor of her face when at last she was settled, that the transfer from bed to chair had cost her.

Not that she'd admit it. "Give me a minute and I'll be ready to race you down the hall," she panted, feebly waving aside their concern.

But Molly knew otherwise, and was so deathly afraid she might have aggravated her mother's hip injury or, even worse, caused major damage, that before she started preparing the fish for dinner, she phoned the clinic. By then regular hours were over, but the answering service promised to pass on her message to Dan who was on call that evening.

When the meal was ready, she and Ariel carried everything upstairs for another picnic in the bedroom: baked salmon steaks with French bread and a salad this time, followed by little fruit tarts Molly had found in a new bakery on Fundy Street where the old shoe repair shop used to be. It was after seven when they finished, and still no call from Dan.

By then Hilda was visibly wilting, though she claimed differently. But there was no missing the effort it took for her to maintain the cheerful zest with which she'd attacked her dinner, and when the phone still hadn't rung at eight, Molly swallowed her pride and went next door.

"I knew you'd never manage without me," Cadie declared smugly, when Molly explained. "Well, don't just stand there looking like lamb on lettuce, girl! Let's get over to your ma's house and put things right."

Whatever else her failings, Cadie had the stamina of a stevedore, and muscles to match under all her flab. After eyeballing the situation for all of three seconds, she swept Hilda up in her arms and had her deposited squarely in the middle of the bed before the patient had a chance to squeak an objection.

"There!" she announced. "Let that be a lesson to you, Hilda Paget. Maybe then you won't be so quick to shut the door on them who's stood by you all these years when certain others chose not to." Then, swinging around to Molly, said, "Anything else you want me to put right while I'm here?"

"No," Molly said, doing her best to sound suitably chastened because she was, in all honesty, grateful. "Thank you, Mrs. Boudelet. I couldn't have managed without you."

"'Course you couldn't!" She swiped one broad palm against the other, hitched her bosom back into place, and nodded to the room at large. "I might only be next door, but it's a sight quicker to pick up the phone the next time you want me here in a hurry, than it is to come racing over the backyard fence in them silly boots. Pity they didn't teach you that at whatever fancy school you went to to learn how to dress like one of them women I see pasted all over the pages of magazines these days! Pity you got your hair cut, as well. Makes you look more like a lad than a woman."

And on that complimentary note, she swept grandly down the stairs and let the back door slam shut behind her with a resounding crash.

At eight-thirty, the good doctor finally showed up. All set to lambaste him for taking so long, Molly changed her mind when she saw the weary slump to his shoulders and said only, "I'm sorry to be bringing you out at this hour."

"That's what I'm here for. Is it Hilda?"

"Yes. Although she won't admit it, she's in a lot of pain and I'm afraid it's my fault."

A faint smile ghosted over his mouth. "What did you do this time, Molly?"

"Lifted her out of bed and sat her in a wheelchair."

"By yourself? Are you crazy?"

"I'm beginning to think so," she said, awash in guilt brought on in part by her mother's misery and in part by his. He looked so tired, so defeated, and surely could have done without having to make another house call on top of whatever else he'd had to cope with that day.

"Did you drop her on the floor?"

"Not quite."

"Oh, brother!" He wiped his hand down his face and started for the stairs. Then, realizing she was hovering in the rear, uncertain whether or not to follow, he threw a glance over his shoulder and said, "Go make a pot of coffee, Molly, and we'll talk after I've examined her. And don't look so woebegone. Hilda's survived a lot worse than this."

He was with her mother nearly half an hour. When he finally joined Molly in the kitchen, she could hardly find the voice to inquire, "Well? How bad is it?"

"Nothing a good night's rest won't cure." He slumped against the counter and watched as she poured the coffee. "I've given her something to ease the discomfort in her hip. Otherwise, she's in remarkably good shape which has, I suspect, less to do with being wrestled around the bed by you than it has with the fact that you're here at all. Her spirits have made a remarkable turnaround."

"Thank goodness! I was so afraid—"

"You should be," he said, cutting short her relief. "If she'd fallen, the outcome would have been vastly different. Didn't we have a deal that you'd wait a couple more weeks before you rushed into any major changes—and even then, only after you'd run them by me?"

"I didn't consider the wheelchair a major change." She bit her lip, annoyed with herself for having so badly miscalculated matters. "I now realize I was wrong."

"If you'd listened to Cadie in the first place, instead of trying to shock her into swallowing her teeth by threatening—"

"What do you know about my run-in with Cadie?"

"Only what your mother told me." He was the one to bite his lip this time, but a smile slipped through anyway. "You realize the whole street will have heard the story by tomorrow, don't you? And that your name will be spattered with a fresh load of mud?"

"I don't care."

"I do."

He was too big for that cramped kitchen. Try though she might, there was no way she could put the safety of distance between them—and the way his voice dropped half an octave when he made his last remark left her very conscious of the danger of letting him get too close.

"Why?" she said, a strange flutter breezing over her.

He reached out and cupped his palm against the side of her neck. His thumb traced a path along her jaw, dipped beneath her chin to stroke lightly down her throat, and the flutter became a cyclone. "Because I'm your friend, whether or not you believe that. And right now, you need me."

She'd needed him for years! He was the reason she'd never found passion with another man. He was the cause of all those sleepless nights, all those secret tears. But she'd rather die than tell him so. "No, I don't," she said, shying away. "I'm used to coping on my own."

"It's okay to ask for help, Molly," he said softly. "There's no rule that says you have to carry this load alone. We all need other people, some of the time."

She thrust a mug of coffee at him. Better he have something else to wrap his hands around than her! "Except you. You've never needed anyone in your life."

"Not true." His chest heaved in a massive sigh as he sank onto a chair. "Nights like tonight, I'd give a lot to be going home to a blazing fire, a table set for two and a wife glad to see me."

She saw then what the dim light in the hall had not revealed: the bleak emptiness in his eyes and the lines of despair bracketing his mouth. Past sins and present virtues notwithstanding, he was neither devil nor god but just a man, as susceptible to pain and sorrow and failure as the next person.

The realization caused something to break loose inside Molly, as if a huge wall of rock encasing her heart suddenly cracked and crumbled into dust. Without thought for the consequences, she leaned over him as he sat at the table and gripped his forearms. "I can't offer you any of those, but I'm here and I'm willing to listen if you think it'll help to talk. What went wrong tonight, Dan, that you're so troubled?"

CHAPTER FOUR

HE MOVED his feet apart just enough to clamp her prisoner between his knees. Though by no means an overtly sexual move, it nevertheless conveyed a familiarity which far exceeded what she'd intended when she'd gone to him so impulsively.

"The summer we met," he said, staring past her as if he were gazing down a tunnel to the past, "isn't a time I remember with any pride. If truth be told, there's a lot of it I don't remember at all. There was you, of course—"

"Among others," she cut in, unreasonably stung by his words. "Given your propensity for chasing women, I suppose I should be flattered you remember me at all. But what's that got to do with tonight?"

"Bear with me, Molly." He grasped her hands and squeezed her fingers absently, leaving her with the sense that although he was there in the flesh, his mind and spirit were miles—and years—away. "That September I took off for Europe with a couple of buddies. We rented a car in Paris and started what we thought would be a two-year jaunt around the world with a tour of France. A week later, on a narrow back road just north of Grenoble, our car sideswiped a family of four out for an afternoon bike ride. The mother had a baby strapped to a seat behind her. A little girl, eighteen months old. She was killed instantly."

"Were you driving the car?"

"No. But I could just as well have been."

"So you decided to become a doctor to ease your con-

58

science? Isn't that a rather convenient cliché, Dan?'' She sounded cold and cynical, she knew, but it was her only defense against the horror crawling over her like tiny insect feet.

All she could think about was Ariel at eighteen months—how plumply adorable she'd been, the way she'd run into Molly's outstretched arms, the sound of her singing in the bath tub—and how dark and worthless life would have become without her. How did a mother ever accept such a loss? Or recover from it?

''I didn't rush out and enroll at the first medical school I came across, if that's what you're implying,'' Dan said. ''But yes, that's when the seed was planted, though I didn't necessarily recognize it at the time.'' He lifted his gaze to meet hers. His eyes, normally as blue as the far depths of the ocean in August, had the bruised look of forget-me-nots carelessly crushed underfoot. ''Seeing that poor mother grieving for her lost baby, and the father helpless to comfort his wife, changed me forever. I realized how much I took life and health for granted.''

The pressure of his knees and the firmness of his hold on her hands continued, but it was the ease with which he touched her emotions that terrified Molly. She wanted to cradle his head to her breast; to stroke his hair and soothe away his misery. Her eyes burned with unshed tears—for those poor people who lost so much in the space of a few seconds, and for him who still carried the burden of their loss eleven years later.

Softly she said, ''Did a baby die tonight, Dan?''

''Two did. A fourteen-year-old girl from The Flats hid in her father's barn and tried to abort a pregnancy. She hemorrhaged to death before I could get her to the hospital.''

''Oh, dear God!''

The Flats, a bleak, wind-scoured stretch of land on which a scattering of farms struggled to survive, lay some ten miles east of Harmony Cove. Its residents, isolated as much by poverty as the elements, were a strange, reclusive lot, fanatical and superstitious in their beliefs, and highly suspicious of outsiders.

"That sort of thing shouldn't still be happening," he said, controlled rage threading the anguish in his voice. "For crying out loud, we're into the twenty-first century! That child had options. If she'd come to the clinic, one of us could have helped her."

"She shouldn't have had to," Molly said, understanding better than he'd ever know how trapped and helpless the poor girl had felt. "She should have been able to turn to her family first, and *they* were the ones who should have brought her to you."

"Would you have gone to your father, if you'd found yourself in the same situation at her age?"

Completely blindsided by the question, she felt the blood rush to her face and a tremor roll over her as devastating as a silent earthquake. He noticed both, and pinned her in another disturbing glance, this one altogether too perceptive.

"I can't imagine being fourteen and pregnant," she said, recklessly sifting about to mine an element of harmless fact from the quicksand of more dangerous truths crowding her mind. "The most I knew about sex at that age was what Alec Livingston tried to teach me when I was ten."

By sheer luck, she'd happened on something guaranteed to lessen the tension swirling between them and divert Dan's curiosity into safer channels. Knees falling slackly apart, he leaned back in stunned amazement. "Alec Livingston tried to get it on with you when you were only ten? The dirty little creep! What did he do, lure you behind the potting shed and offer to show you his etchings?''

''The lobster shed, actually, and he wasn't quite that sophisticated.'' At last free to remove herself from the drugging pleasure of his hold without making an issue of it, she picked up their coffee mugs and rinsed them out at the sink. ''Potting sheds aren't a common site on Wharf Street, in case you haven't noticed. We tend to stick to more basic construction, like keeping a roof over our own heads. It's only people like you, living on the lake, who worry about providing housing for plants.''

''Oh, no, you don't, Molly!'' In the reflection of the window above the sink, she saw him get up from the chair and lope toward her. ''You're not wriggling off the hook that easily.''

Feigning innocence, she said, ''You want more coffee?''

''You know damn well that's not what I'm talking about. Exactly what sort of stunt did the Livingston boy try to pull?''

She was wedged between Dan and the counter, hemmed in by the stove on one side, and the back door on the other. Not exactly the most romantic place in the world, but certainly one fraught with enough perilous potential that she went weak at the knees.

His body heat entwined with hers. His breath winnowed over her mouth in a phantom kiss that left her craving the real flesh-and-blood encounter. The very pores of her skin pulsed with longing for his touch.

She must be mad!

Lifting her gaze to his, she said baldly, ''He offered to show me what he so delicately termed his 'pecker' if I'd let him see my 'dingle'!''

She'd hoped to break the mood, and she succeeded. Dan's body gave a sudden heave as if he were trying not to lose his lunch, except it was a burst of laughter he attempted to contain. "And how," he choked out, turning his head aside as if he thought that could disguise his unholy glee, "did you respond?"

"I plowed my fist in his nose as hard as I could and sent him home screaming, with blood pouring down his face. And if you're interested in the sequel, his mother came to my father with the story of how I'd tried to lead her darling boy down the primrose path to ruin, then beaten him up when he refused to cooperate. Rotten Alec was treated like a martyr, and I was condemned for everything from fornication to assault."

"Oh, Molly!" He was laughing so hard, his eyes were tearing.

"I'm glad you find it so amusing," she snapped, recalling the injustice of it all as if it had happened only yesterday. *Hussy!* John Paget had roared, wielding his belt with vigor and leaving bright red welts on her leg. *Slut!* "But if you'd had a father like mine, you'd be laughing on the other side of your face! I know exactly how that poor girl felt tonight—alone, afraid, defenseless, with no one to take her side."

Abruptly sobering, Dan said, "That's the tragedy of it. She didn't have to be alone."

"Really? I don't know how you arrive at that conclusion. Obviously she didn't feel she could confide in her parents. And I haven't heard you make mention of the baby's father. Perhaps if he'd stepped forward and taken his share of responsibility for the pregnancy, there might never have been an abortion attempt to begin with."

"Perhaps not," he murmured, and surprised her with a touch to her cheek; a whisper of a caress which traveled in languid seduction from the tip of her ear to the underside of her jaw. "When did you become so wise, my Molly?"

"I'm not your Molly," she said, but her tone carried not a shred of conviction. Worse, despite her best efforts to prevent it, her eyes fell closed, weighted by the memory of a time when she'd been *all* his and held nothing of herself in reserve.

She heard his sharply indrawn breath. Sensed the awareness suddenly humming through him, as if he, too, remembered the intimacy they'd once shared. She felt his breath again on her mouth, warmer this time, and close enough that it left a faint damp cloud on her lips. And would have lifted her face for the kiss she knew was coming if another voice hadn't defused the electricity charging the air.

"Mommy," Ariel croaked plaintively from the doorway, "my throat hurts."

Molly's eyes flew open only to find themselves captured by Dan's for a long, tense second. Then, with enviable calm, he stepped away and turned to speak to her daughter. "When did it start, pumpkin?"

"Just now." Ariel swallowed audibly and whimpered with pain. "When I woke up."

He swung back to Molly again. "Want me to take a look?"

"Absolutely not!" Blind fear getting the better of the rational judgment with which she'd normally have responded to such an offer, she ducked past him to shield Ariel from his too-observant inspection. Oh, it had been a mistake to let him linger in the house; a mistake to have called on him at all! She couldn't afford to risk his coming into contact with her child so frequently. "Don't you dare come near her!"

She didn't need his raised eyebrows or calm, "I'm offering to give her a medical examination, Molly, not abscond with her," to know that she'd overreacted and it hadn't gone unnoticed.

Collecting herself with difficulty, she replied, "I'm not suggesting you were. I just don't want to take advantage of you, that's all. You've put in enough hours for one day, and a sore throat is hardly a major emergency. Ariel's a mouth breather when she sleeps and quite often wakes up like this. It's nothing that a glass of water won't cure."

"She looks a little flushed to me. Could be she's running a temperature."

"Children always look flushed when they've been sleeping."

"If you say so." He paused a moment as though undecided whether or not to pursue the matter, then shrugged and collected his medical bag from the table. "I can't force you to let me examine her, but I strongly suggest you keep a close eye on her. I assume you flew here?"

"We did."

"Then you must be aware that all that recycled air in those pressurized jet cabins is a breeding ground for respiratory infections. If she's not noticeably improved by the morning, don't fool around. Get her to a doctor—and it doesn't have to be me, if that's what's holding you back. Marjorie Anderson is one of my partners and she's excellent with children."

"It's not that I don't have confidence in you, Dan. No offence intended, really."

"None taken," he said easily. "We never did talk about your agenda for Hilda and now obviously isn't a good time to get into it, so I'll be off. But I would like to go over whatever other harebrained ideas you're cooking up on her behalf before you put them into practice.''

"I already promised you I'll call, and I will."

"Make it soon," he said darkly. "Or I'll call you."

She was so eager to get rid of him, she damn near slammed the door while he had still had one leg inside the house. And he'd bet money he knew why. Without saying a word, she'd given away her secret. It had to do with Ariel—and him.

Putting two and two together and coming up with four wasn't difficult. The flimsy web of lies she'd concocted to throw him off the scent weren't nearly as convincing as the rank terror which sent her into overdrive whenever he came within spitting distance of her or her daughter.

In hindsight, everything added up.

She'd been horrified to find he was a presence in her mother's life. Without waiting to discover whether or not he was fit to be let loose with a stethoscope, she'd threatened to have him removed from the case. She'd defended that poor child from The Flats with a vehemence out of all proportion to her involvement in the case. And she'd just about broken the sound barrier leaping between him and Ariel when he'd offered to take a look at the kid's sore throat—scarcely something to be interpreted as an invasive medical procedure!

Pausing next to his car, he inhaled a lungful of the sharp night air. From the corner of his eye, he saw a starched lace curtain lift at the living room window of the house he'd just left. She was watching him, wanting to be sure he didn't decide to come back and start probing and poking around into matters best left untouched.

Too late, Molly! The proverbial cat is out of the bag

and there's no stuffing it back in again. The question is, what are we going to do about it?

Deep in thought, he climbed into the car and sat a moment, staring down the hill. A floodlamp on a post at the end of the dock spilled a circle of yellow light over the lobster traps piled next to the wooden shed behind which Alec Livingston had met his comeuppance with Molly.

And now, it seemed, so had Dan Cordell. The only difference was, it had taken eleven years to catch up with him. The complications it entailed didn't exactly enthrall him. Seeing Molly again had been disturbing enough. Until she resurfaced, he'd been happy with Summer.

A doctor's daughter, Summer well understood the demands of the profession. Married to her, he'd come home at night to orderly tranquillity and tasteful comfort, regardless of how late it might be. There'd be a table set with crystal and china. Fine wine and gourmet meals. Classical music playing softly in the background, and a leaping fire to brighten black winter evenings.

Eventually there'd be children, two at the most. A boy and a girl, with perfect, healthy bodies he could hug tight and thank God for, on those days he'd tended to some undernourished sickly baby who'd never know the luxury of sweet-smelling sheets or a mother with petal-soft hands to soothe away the night fears.

It was all there waiting for him, and the only thing he had to do was reach out and grasp it. More than that, he just had to say the word and he'd be out of the clinic and into her father's nice, clean, white-collar practice where patients knew better than to drag a man out of bed in the middle of the night.

Forget infections neglected so long that they required major intervention to bring them under control. Forget the chronic winter cough which became pneumonia and left a two-year-old fighting for its life. Forget botched abortions in dirty barns. The rich didn't wait until two in the morning to call for professional help. They didn't try to cope by themselves with ancient remedies which often made illness worse. They weren't buried in such awe of doctors that they turned to one only as a last resort.

He could, if he chose, abandon his commitment to the hopeless and the helpless. He could let some other idealist take up the slack for a change, secure in the knowledge that he'd done his bit for the underprivileged.

But how to turn his back on a leggy ten-year-old with big brown eyes and long dark braids, and a smile which, one day, would steal a man's heart and never give it back? How to bury the memories hounding him of the summer that child had been conceived?

The fling with Molly had begun innocently enough, about a week after she'd cut her hand at the restaurant. She'd been assigned to the late shift and he'd noticed how tired she looked. But he'd noticed other things, too: the full, passionate mouth, the big, dark, defiant eyes; the lush curve of her breasts beneath the green striped tunic of her uniform, the delicious sun-kissed length of her legs exposed by the midthigh hem of the little green skirt. And his motives hadn't been nearly as pure as he'd made them out to be when he'd offered to give her a ride home after work.

"It's a beautiful night," he said, when she came out to where he sat astride the Harley at the back entrance to the restaurant. "What say we go for a spin before I take you home?"

She eyed the bike warily and sensing she was about to refuse, he'd added, "We'll make it short. Just out to The Point and back. Half an hour at the most. And I promise not to speed. You'll be perfectly safe."

She debated a moment longer, then allowed an impish smile to slip through. Eyes flashing beneath the sweep of her lashes, she said, "Why not?"

She climbed aboard, wrapped her arms around his waist and laughed aloud as he peeled away from the curb. Within minutes, they'd cleared the town and were headed along the winding road up the cliff to The Point overlooking the Bay of Fundy. At that hour, close to eleven, it was deserted. The sky was peppered with stars, the air still and silent except for the distant swish of the sea.

Without waiting for him, she slipped off the bike, climbed over the safety barrier, and standing at the very edge of the cliff, raised her arms as though embracing the night. Released from the netting that was a standard part of The Ivy Tree uniform, her hair streamed down her back, black as night, smooth as water.

Joining her, he said, "Do you always live this dangerously?"

"I thought you said I'd be safe."

"You were, on the bike. Right now though, you're dancing with disaster. Come away from the edge, for Pete's sake. You're giving me the willies."

"I'm not afraid."

"I am," he said, taking her arm. Her skin was cool and smooth as cream; her profile, dimly illuminated by starlight, mysterious and alluring. "I don't fancy having to face your parents and tell them you fell a thousand feet to your death."

"They wouldn't care," she said. "At least, my father wouldn't. He'd be glad he was rid of me."

There'd been not a hint of self-pity in her words, just such a calm statement of fact that he, who'd never once questioned his own parents' devotion to him, felt a pang of compassion. "Come away," he said again, taking her by the hand and drawing her back to sit beside him on the safety rail. ''You're too young and beautiful to give in to thoughts like that.''

''I don't want your pity,'' she informed him tartly. ''There's no need to butter me up with compliments.'' But when he'd slipped his arm around her waist and pulled her to him, she leaned against him with a long, suppressed sigh which belied her claim.

The women he knew wore silk and cashmere. They smelled of Chanel or Paloma Picasso. Their nails and hair were professionally maintained. They drove European sports cars and spent part of every winter in the Bahamas.

Molly had changed out of her uniform into a cheap cotton skirt and short-sleeved blouse. Her hair fell in an untamed swath over her shoulders. Neither it nor her skin carried any hint of perfume except the scent which he came to associate always with her: line-dried clothes, plain soap and the wild thyme he later learned she sewed into little pouches and hung in her closet. She would not have merited a second glance from the crowd he ran with, yet her unadorned beauty stirred him to a wanting different from anything he'd known before.

He inched closer. Felt the warmth of her thigh melting against his, the side swell of her breast pressing against his ribs. When he nudged at her lips with his mouth, she lifted her face willingly and let him kiss her.

He didn't know quite what he'd expected. Prim bashfulness, perhaps, or the coy little games of innocence other women he'd known liked to play, pretending to be shocked by a kiss but so ready to drop their drawers that a guy seldom got the chance to do it for them. Either way, he figured he could handle it.

For once, though, he was taken totally by surprise. Oh sure, the innocence was there, except it was the real thing.

No acting, no games, just artless, unfeigned rapture. And that was what really ambushed him. Her mouth opened like a tropical bloom: sweet, hot, and fragrant with passion. Her tongue entwined instinctively with his, ingenuous and eager.

She made a little sound deep in her throat, halfway between a sigh and a moan. He felt a flush creep over her skin. Her hands clutched mindlessly at his T-shirt; tightened into fists against his chest. And the desire circling the perimeter of his consciousness like a distant thunderstorm settled in his groin, leaving him painfully constricted in his narrow-fitting chinos.

Her blouse closed down the front. Undoing the buttons was a piece of cake; slipping his hand inside the cotton cup of her bra something he accomplished in a matter of seconds. When he found her nipple, she bit down on his lip—a sharp, involuntary pinch that softened into a gasp of pleasure. "Ahh…!" she breathed, her head falling back in surrender.

In retrospect, he liked to think he wouldn't have let matters go much further, at least not on the first date, if that's what it could be called. But she hadn't had nearly enough. Slipping the straps of her bra down her arms, she cushioned her breasts in her hands and with a lack of self-consciousness he found moving beyond words, offered them for him to sample. They gleamed faintly in the gloom, olive-skinned and so perfect that it was enough to make him lose whatever speck of decency he had left.

Before she had time to collect herself, he'd had one hand up her skirt and the other yanking open his fly. Pulling her astride his lap, he teased her flesh with the tip of his. She was wet and hot and so helpless to suppress the pleasure of his touch that she started to cry.

But when he went to withdraw, she clung to him and

begged him not to stop. She knotted her fingers in his hair, dragged his lips to her breast, and gave a hiccuping sob when he drew her nipple into his mouth.

Half mad with desire, he'd driven into her, so close to the edge that when she wrapped her long legs around his waist and tilted her hips to meet his thrusts, he exploded in a burst of passion that left him groaning.

By some miracle, she came, too, in a series of inarticulate little cries and contractions that left her quivering around him long after he'd spilled inside her. It had been the first of many times that they'd made love and the only time he hadn't used a condom.

Recalling that summer now, in the dark, chill confines of his car, he found himself hard for her all over again while, on the other side of town, Summer sat alone in her apartment with his ring on her finger.

And he, louse that he was, could focus only on one thing: earthy, wild, uninhibited passion with Molly versus refined sex with Summer who never had a hair out of place and conducted herself with the dignity of a duchess, even between the sheets.

Disgusted, both with his past and present performance, he rolled down the window and roared off up Wharf Street with the bitter Atlantic wind howling around his ears. It would serve him right if he caught pneumonia. It was no less than he deserved.

But he needed to clear his head before he did or said something so rash that he ruined three lives.

Summer deserved better than to be tossed aside on a whim. He had to tread carefully around Molly, or she'd grow suspicious and take flight. Most of all, he had to keep his distance from Ariel until he'd figured out the least damaging way to integrate her into his life. Because there was no doubt in his mind that she was his daughter, and no question but that, one way or another, he was going to fill the empty shoes of fatherhood and be there for his little girl. And if doing so lost him the respect and admiration of those whose opinion he'd hitherto valued, that was their tough luck.

CHAPTER FIVE

MOLLY lay awake most of the night, figuring out her next move. Above all else, she *had* to put distance between Dan and Ariel, and by far the safest way to do that would have been to take her daughter and climb aboard the first flight headed back to Seattle.

There were only three problems: her West Coast address was a matter of record at Harmony Cove General Hospital, which meant Dan could trace her easily should he choose to do so; she couldn't leave her mother; and Hilda was in no shape to make such a long trip, even if Molly could have persuaded her to undertake it. Seventeen Wharf Street had been her home since the day she'd crossed the threshold as John Paget's twenty-two-year-old bride, nearly fifty years ago.

Looming larger than these obstacles, though, was the memory of Dan as he'd looked after he left the house the previous night, standing so long in the ice-black cold that he might have been cast in stone. There'd been something deeply disturbing in his posture; something so utterly still and reflective that the hair on the back of Molly's neck had bristled with premonition. Gripped by an overwhelming uneasiness based on nothing but instinct, she'd remained hidden behind the curtains in the living room long after he'd driven away.

The first hint of dawn left the sky beyond the harbor streaked with orange before she finally fell asleep, but by then she'd come up with a plan which, unless she'd missed something vital, offered at least a temporary solution.

Over midmorning coffee in her mother's bedroom, she asked, "How attached are you to this house, Momma? Could you ever see yourself living somewhere else?"

"It's not something I've ever given any thought to," Hilda said, after a pause. "I know it's no palace, Moll, but it's familiar and that means a lot when you get to be my age."

Taking advantage of the fact that, though her question hadn't been received with unqualified enthusiasm, nor had it been rejected out of hand, Molly said, "If it meant Ariel and I could stay with you a little longer, would you consider a temporary move to something more spacious? Because you must know, Mom, that as long as you're confined to this room, it's going to take you twice as long to get your strength back. Even if we set your bed up downstairs, it'd be a stop-gap solution at best. You need regular physiotherapy and that's not going to happen as long as you're housebound."

"If moving would mean I'd get to keep my two girls with me, I'd go to the moon, you know that. But how can you stay here, when you've got a shop to run in Seattle and Ariel's supposed to be in school?"

"I left my friend Elaine in charge of the shop. She already looks after inventory and suppliers, so I know it's in good hands. As for Ariel's schooling, I've arranged for a tutor to come in four hours every day from Monday to Friday, to keep her out of mischief and up-to-date on her studies. Which leaves the next move quite literally up to you, Mom. So what do you say?"

Hilda, who'd been reclining against the headboard and apparently ruminating on the possibilities opening up to her, suddenly bolted upright. "You're not planning to shove me into a retirement home, are you? Because I can tell you right now, Molly, I'm not ready for that! I'm not giving up my independence, just because of a flight of stairs and a house that's not as big and fancy as you think it should be."

"If I was proposing shoving you into a retirement home, there'd be no need for me to stay here, would there?" Willing herself to patience, Molly buried a sigh. "I'm not my father, Mom. I don't ride roughshod over other people without a thought for their rights or opinions."

Somewhat reassured, her mother sank back against the pillows. "Well, if it's not an old folks' home you're thinking of, exactly what *have* you got up your sleeve?"

"The Harmony Cove Inn."

"The Inn?" Hilda's faded blue eyes grew large as saucers in her thin face. "If it were summer, I'd think you'd had a touch too much sun! Even if I could afford it, they'd never let me in there unless I wanted to scrub floors!"

"*I* can afford it, Mom. And it'll be a cold day in hell before I let you scrub anybody's floors, including your own, ever again."

"I wouldn't be comfortable—"

"Yes, you would. That's the whole point. You wouldn't have to cope with stairs, you'd have room to wheel around in the chair until you're strong enough to try a walker. If you did nothing else, you could sit in the lobby and people-watch, which is a sight more than you're able to do now. And it's not as if you'll be alone. Ariel and I will be right there with you."

"Well, when you put it like that..." She ruminated some more, but Molly could tell from the slow smile creeping over her mother's face, that the idea had taken firm root. "Heavenly days, what's Cadie Boudelet going to think when she hears!"

They made the move two weeks later, on a Saturday kissed by the first real breath of spring. On the Thursday before, Molly broke the news to Dan after he'd finished the second of his semiweekly house calls.

"What's the holdup?" she inquired testily, when he started to raise objections. "You've just finished telling me you can't believe the improvement in my mother's health and mental outlook. You agreed days ago that she'll benefit from the change. And now that I have the van, I'll be able to bring her to the clinic for her checkups, thereby leaving you with one less home visit to make in a schedule already flowing over at the seams. Admit it, Dan. There's nothing to be gained by her staying in this decrepit old place, and nothing she's getting here that she can't have at the Inn."

He stroked the ball of his thumb over his mouth a moment, obviously considering the merit of her arguments. Then, exhaling a long breath, said, "I guess you've got a point, but it's going to cost a small fortune, you know."

"You stick to doctoring and leave me to worry about the money," she said sharply.

He shrugged and stuffed his stethoscope into his pocket. "If you say so. But if I might be permitted to ask, how do you plan to get her from her bedroom to the van—piggyback her downstairs, or parachute her out the bedroom window?"

"I haven't quite decided, but I'm sure I'll manage."

"I applaud your independence, Molly," he said, "but if I might make a suggestion without getting my head bitten off, let me arrange for an ambulance to transport her to her new digs. That way, I'm less likely to be called to emergency to fix a few more broken bones should you not manage as well as you anticipate.''

"Thank you," she said starchily, wishing she'd thought of it herself instead of trying to figure out a way to get Cadie Boudelet to lend a hand without having to grovel for favors. "That's very kind of you."

He bathed her in a grin so engaging, she practically reeled from its dismaying effect on her heart rate. "That's me, all right. A regular boy scout! So, I guess the next time I see you, it'll be at the clinic."

"Yes," she said. "I'll make an appointment for Monday so that you can see for yourself that she's none the worse for moving up in the world."

In fact, she ran into him again on the Sunday, and it wasn't a pleasant encounter.

The Harmony Cove Inn, a gracious two-storied establishment built around the beginning of the nineteenth century, sprawled over the crest of exclusive Wolfe Avenue, commanding a stunning view of the harbor and distant Lighthouse Island. Surrounded by vast gardens manicured to a fare-thee-well in summer, it had played host to countless heads of state over the years. Century-old maple and elm dotted its lawns, mullioned windows winked from its weathered stone walls, massive beams supported its ceilings.

As the ambulance drew up at the main entrance, with Molly and Ariel following in the van, smoke curled from the tall chimneys silhouetted against the bright blue sky. A clump of birch trees threw purple shadows over the last melting clumps of snow. Pale green tips of daffodils poked through the freshly turned earth under the shelter of the bowed front windows.

So overwhelmed that she was on the verge of tears,

Hilda reached out to grasp Molly's hand as they waited to check in at the front desk. "I've lived in this town all my life, Moll," she exclaimed, gazing in awe at the charming lobby with its bowls of fresh flowers, ornately framed antique prints, and hardwood floors worn to satin smoothness by the passage of thousands of feet over the last two hundred years, "but this is the first time I've ever seen anything as grand as this."

"It *is* perfect." But unlike the things which drew her mother's admiration, what Molly noticed was the doorman in his gray uniform, the clerk behind the desk and most of all the arched wrought-iron gate which barred people enjoying the public rooms from invading the privacy of resident guests. Safety barriers, every one, standing between her and Dan. Between Dan and Ariel. He wouldn't be dropping in here, whenever the mood took him, and poking his nose into matters best left alone.

She'd booked a suite on the main floor, a two-bedroom affair with a sitting room which opened onto a sun-drenched private courtyard. As the weather improved, her mother would be able to sit out there and enjoy the fresh air.

Until then, two comfortable wing chairs and a small sofa flanking a tiled fireplace equipped with gleaming brass andirons beckoned invitingly. An antique cabinet in one corner held a television set and stereo; a pedestal table and four chairs stood next to the window. The entire main floor of the house on Wharf Street would have fit in there, and still left room to spare.

The bedrooms were equally spacious, the two twin beds in each piled with feather pillows and traditional hand-stitched quilts reminiscent of the ones her mother and Cadie Boudelet used to make every winter. A selection of lotions, shampoo, hand-milled French soap and thick, velvety towels stocked the en suite bathrooms. No expense had been spared in providing for the comfort of guests.

It made the perfect retreat even though, as Dan had predicted, it cost plenty. But for Molly, her mother's pleasure at being surrounded by so many fine things made it worth every cent. Here Hilda could recover in comfort, and Molly's own secret remain safe.

"We'll have our meals brought to the suite today," she decided, realizing that, when lunchtime came, one reason her mother was reluctant to be seen in the dining room stemmed less from her being in a wheelchair than from embarrassment with her clothes.

There had never been money to spare for extras, or occasion to wear anything glamorous, with the result that Hilda's wardrobe was basic, to put it mildly. So while she napped in the afternoon and Ariel worked on a jigsaw puzzle, Molly went shopping, returning to the Inn just as dusk fell with enough boxes and bags that she needed a bellhop to help carry everything to the suite.

"There's no point in feeling like a queen if you don't look the part, Momma," she decreed, overriding Hilda's protests of extravagance. "And some of this stuff's for Ariel, as well."

"Not that thing, I hope," her mother said, eyeing a flowing robe of scarlet satin trimmed with marabou feathers at the hem and wrists. "Your father used to forbid me buying you anything that was red. He thought it brought out the lust in men."

Deciding that probably had a lot to do with why her mother stuck to black or brown, thereby shielding herself from his unwelcome attentions, Molly stroked the offending garment, loving its rich, soft texture. "Don't worry, Mom, this one's for me, and I can assure you there won't be any men beating down my door with evil intent on their minds. You and Ariel are the only two people who'll see me wearing it.''

At seven on Sunday evening, they left the suite in high spirits and wound their way along the window-lined gallery connecting the private rooms to the public area, to dine in style in the Cranberry Room. Ariel skipped ahead, dark braids bouncing, full skirt swirling around her long legs, leaving her mother and grandmother to follow at a more sedate pace.

Hilda wore a blue wool dress a shade deeper than her eyes, and what used to be her Sunday-best shoes. With her hair freshly washed and curled, a touch of lipstick on her mouth and a hint of blusher to relieve her pale cheeks, she looked like a new woman.

The lilt to her voice, the liveliness in her expression, were worlds removed from the woebegone picture she'd presented just a few weeks before, and watching her, Molly knew a pang of regret for all the wasted years. That a little loving attention and a new dress were all it took to reverse the neglect left her ragged with guilt.

"In case I haven't said it in so many words, I love you, Momma, and I'm sorry I waited so long to come home and act the way a daughter should,'' she murmured, touching her mother's shoulder.

Hilda reached up and patted her hand consolingly. "You spend too much time dwelling on past mistakes, child. You've got to find a way to forgive yourself, and me, and all the other people who haven't done right by you over the years. You've never said who Ariel's father is and I'm not asking you to name him now because it doesn't matter anymore, but I will say this: I've often thought the reason you've never married is that you can't let go of the past. But not all men are like him or your father, and I'd dearly like to see you happy with a good and decent husband. It's what every mother wants for her daughter.''

At that point, they reached the wrought-iron gate, and things started going downhill the minute they passed through into the main lobby of the Inn.

''I don't need a husband. I'm happy with things just the way they are,'' Molly said stiffly, then casting a glance at Ariel who'd noticed a display of Victorian dolls in a glass-fronted cabinet and lingered to inspect them, put an end to the discussion by calling out, ''Ariel, sweetheart, we're going in for dinner now. You can look at the dolls later.''

Always willing to please, Ariel spun around with the coltish exuberance of youth which never failed to amaze Molly, and barreled full force into a group of people emerging from the coat-check room.

''Watch where you're going, young lady!'' one of the women exclaimed in tones of well-bred annoyance, and with sinking horror, Molly realized the speaker was Yvonne Cordell, that Dan was with her, as was his father, another couple of about the same vintage as his parents, and a younger woman closer to his age who seemed to be the only female among them who cared that a child might be hurt.

She reached down to help a mortified Ariel just as Molly bolted to the rescue. But Dan was faster than either of them and grasping Ariel by the waist, swung her to her feet and muttered something in her ear which turned her incipient tears into a giggle.

Of course, he had to look devastating in a navy suit and a shirt so white it matched his smile. And of course, the kind younger woman who wore an engagement ring sporting a diamond solitaire the size of Ariel's thumb nail, belonged to him, as anyone with eyes could tell just from the way she leaned against him and tucked her hand under his arm.

She was tiny, coming only to his shoulder, and possessed of the quiet, understated beauty which only the rich ever seemed to acquire. "I hope your little girl's not hurt," she said with genuine sweetness. "She took quite a fall, I'm afraid."

"I'm sure she's perfectly fine," Molly replied, snatching Ariel out of Dan's reach and knowing she sounded about as charming as a black widow spider on the hunt. "Come along, Ariel. Your grandmother's waiting for us."

But Hilda hadn't spent most of the last two days practicing spinning the wheels on her chair for the sheer fun of it, and she wasn't waiting for anyone. "Dr. Cordell!" she cooed, waving to catch his attention before Molly could prevent her, and rolling across the polished floor in a burst of speed which had Yvonne Cordell shying away like a nervous thoroughbred. "Guess you never expected to see me here, now did you?"

Excusing himself from his party, Dan came to where Hilda sat beaming with delight and Molly stood with what she feared was a sickly grimace plastered on her face.

"Glad to see you out and looking so well, Hilda," he said, oozing just the right blend of charm and concern. "Don't overdo it, though, okay? I'd hate to have you suffer a relapse."

"I haven't felt this well in longer than I can remember," she confided. "My Molly's given me a new lease on life."

"Has she?" His gaze rested briefly on Molly, then flickered away indifferently. "That's good to hear."

Unsure whether to feel relieved or insulted at being so summarily dismissed, she said, "Don't let us keep you from your family and friends, Doctor."

"I won't," he said, turning away. "Enjoy your evening."

"You were almost rude to that sweet man," her mother chided, curls bobbing in the breeze as Molly fairly raced to get her in the dining room before anything else untoward occurred. "What's gotten into you, Molly?"

"I don't like him."

"Why ever not? What's he ever done to you?"

Dear heaven, Momma, she thought distractedly, *if you only knew!* "Nothing," she replied, then heaved another sigh of defeated exasperation as the maitre d' stepped forward to greet them.

"Hello, Molly," Alec Livingston crowed, an altogether too knowing smirk on his doughy, freckled face. "I heard you were back in town."

"It's Alec from down the street," her mother supplied helpfully. "You remember him, don't you, Molly?"

"Oh, yes." Would that she could forget!

"He used to pull your braids when you were Ariel's age."

He used to do other unpleasant things, too! "I remember, Mother," she said, tempted to grind her heel down hard on his instep. Fixing him in a cold stare instead, she settled for, "Show us to our table, please."

"Sure thing, Molly. Is it just you and your ma and the little girl?"

"That's why I reserved a table for three."

His insolence almost palpable, he led the way to a table at one side of the fireplace and slapped down three menus. "Just checking. Thought maybe your husband might be here, as well."

As if word hadn't spread the length and breadth of Wharf Street that she'd come back with no visible sign of a father for the child she'd brought with her!

Dan and his group showed up in the doorway just then and for once Molly was almost grateful to see him. At least it spared her having to stomach any more of Alec Livingston's snide remarks. Just about falling over himself, he rushed to attend to the new arrivals.

"Good evening, sir, madam," he gushed in plummy tones, bowing to the senior Dr. Cordell and his wife as if they were of royal lineage. "Such a pleasure to welcome you and your guests to the Cranberry Room again. If you'll follow me please, I have your table waiting."

His obsequious deferral to them stood in glaring contrast to his blatant lack of respect toward Molly. But then, wasn't that the way he'd always been—belligerent from the cradle and never happier than when he was bullying someone he perceived to be weaker than him, and a fawning bootlicker to anyone with clout or social prestige? And shouldn't she be used to such treatment on her home turf by now?

Hiding behind her menu, Hilda eyed her curiously and whispered, "You don't like him, either, do you?"

"I detest him," Molly said, making no attempt to lower her voice. "He is beyond contempt. What do you fancy for dinner, Mother?"

But Hilda was too occupied putting two and two together and coming up with five, to care about food. Glance swinging furtively from Molly to Ariel to Alec, she said in a shocked voice, "Oh, Molly! Is he...*you know who?*"

"Good grief, no! Never in a month of Sundays!" So exasperated she was ready to scream, Molly rolled her eyes and decided she'd opt for room service in future, if this was any indication of what dining in public entailed. "Honestly, Mom, give me credit for having *some* taste!

Let's try to forget he exists, shall we, and decide what we're going to order for dinner?''

If Summer epitomized cool, calm serenity, Molly represented fire and fury about to erupt. Magnificent in a cherry-red pant suit with a gold choker necklace at her throat, all she needed was a spear in one hand to complete the picture of a warrior princess about to do battle with her enemies. Sadly she appeared to view him among their number.

"You know, Daniel, it's untoward to allow your patients to intrude on your personal time and you really shouldn't encourage the kind of familiarity that woman displayed,'' his mother declared, clearly having noticed the way his glance kept straying to the table on the other side of the fireplace. "Those people are not our type.''

Sure both Molly and her mother must have heard, Dan felt a flush of annoyance run under his skin. "They're my type,'' he snapped. "I'd be hard-pressed to make a living without them.''

"Doesn't have to be that way, son,'' Henry Winslow boomed. "There's room for your name on the letterhead in my office whenever you're ready to take me up on my offer.''

"Perhaps after we're married, but not now, Daddy,'' Summer said softly. "Dan is very committed to the Eastside Clinic, and I'm sure his patients are as devoted to him as he is to them.''

"His father was dedicated, too, darling,'' Yvonne said, the frozen distaste in her expression melting into warm approval as she swung her gaze from Molly to Summer, "but he never permitted his patients to forget their place, which is more than can be said for the management here at the Inn. I never thought to find myself sitting down to dine with patrons whom, for want of a better word, I'm forced to describe as commonplace. That young woman," she decreed, surveying Molly over the top of her half-glasses, "needs to teach her hooligan child some manners if she seriously expects to take her out in public. The girl almost knocked me off my feet and didn't even have the grace to apologize."

The upsurge of emotion his mother's latest broadside evoked took Dan completely by surprise. Rage mingled with pain, and he was hard-pressed not to create a scene which would have embarrassed everyone, including himself. Choked, he said, "She's just a kid, for Pete's sake!"

"So were you, once. But you never behaved as she did."

A fat lot you know, Mother! he thought. My sins were a hell of a lot worse than tripping over my own feet and I was years older than my daughter at the time.

Summer, sensing his anger, laid a placating hand over his. The diamond he'd given her winked in the candle-light. "Never mind, Dan," she murmured. "It's not important."

"Exactly," Nancy Winslow chimed in. "We're here to celebrate Yvonne's birthday, so can we please forget about people who bear no relevance to the occasion, and just concentrate on having a good time?"

But it *was* important, damn it, and Dan *did* mind—more deeply than he'd ever have guessed. It took a major toll on his self-discipline not to pound his fist on the table and bellow, "That's *my* child you're dismissing as irrelevant, and the mother and grandmother of *my* child you're rejecting as being of no account!"

At liberty to do no such thing, he wrestled instead with the sobering realization that he was no longer in charge of the events shaping his life. Meanwhile, the conversation around him turned to more agreeable topics, and the unpleasantness was forgotten as if it had never arisen. And while, in the past, he might not have condoned such an attitude, he wouldn't normally have let it get under his skin to the extent that it did now.

These were, after all, the kind of social situations to which he'd been born and bred. One didn't allow inconsequential irritations to spoil one's pleasures. And there was little doubt that the prevailing opinion at his table was that Molly and her entourage were about as insignificant as gnats.

Only Summer seemed sympathetic to his mood, and that merely compounded his problems. Because if he'd learned nothing else from the heated exchange just ended, it was that keeping his connection to Ariel a secret was out of the question.

He hadn't been there to bandage her scraped knees the first time she fell off a bike, or comfort her when she woke up from a bad dream, or sit up the whole night when she had croup. But he'd be damned if he was going to remain silent while others criticized her. He couldn't and he wouldn't.

He owed it to himself and to Ariel to establish beyond any doubt that he was her father, and if that meant confronting Molly a lot sooner than he'd anticipated and run the risk of her hightailing it back to the West Coast, it was a chance he was prepared to take.

The drawback was, the fallout would hurt Summer. And that was the last thing he wanted, because she didn't deserve it.

CHAPTER SIX

AFTER her mother and Ariel were in bed, Molly relaxed in a hot bath for half an hour, then slipped into the red satin robe, put her feet up in the sitting room, and settled down to watch a movie on TV. But neither the figures on the screen nor the words coming out of their mouths could displace the humiliation which had turned dinner into a farce.

Bad enough that she'd had to suffer through a dozen subtle displays of affection between Dan and his fiancée. Not once during their two-month affair had he flaunted *their* relationship before the whole world. Instead they'd sneaked around, meeting in the alley behind The Ivy Tree after dark, or in some out-of-the-way spot beyond the town limits. And only once had he been foolish—or cruel—enough to subject her to his family's scrutiny.

At seventeen, she'd convinced herself that he'd wanted to keep their association secret for *her* sake, to spare her reputation. It was why he often took her to a motel some fifty miles down the coast. Then, one night, they'd fallen asleep after making love, and not woken until nearly three in the morning. When she got home, she'd climbed over the woodshed roof and in through her bedroom window, only to find her father waiting for her, his leather belt swinging from one hand.

She hadn't cared. What she and Dan shared had made it all worthwhile. Their lovemaking had been the stuff that poets wrote about; something which had transcended the ordinary and lifted her beyond her father's tyranny. For years afterward, she'd comforted herself with the notion that if Dan *had* been the kind to settle down, it would have been with her.

At twenty-eight she knew differently. He was capable of entering into as deep and lasting a commitment as any other man. But it had to be with the right kind of woman, one he could parade in public. And if, in some backwater, not-very-bright corner of her mind, Molly hadn't been willing to recognize the fact before, she'd certainly had it rammed down her throat tonight.

Add to that the insulting behavior of the other women in his party, and it was small wonder that, when at last their main course had been cleared away, she did her best to talk her mother into having dessert and coffee brought to the suite, on the grounds that she was looking a bit worn.

"But I feel better than I have in months," her mother had protested.

"Even so, Dr. Cordell's right," she'd argued, just about gagging on having to speak his name, let alone support anything he'd said. "You shouldn't overdo things on your first day out. And regardless, I want Ariel to get an early night tonight because I know she must be tired."

Hilda glanced past the dining room's open double doors to the lobby where Ariel had her nose pressed up against the cabinet holding the dolls. "She doesn't look tired to me."

"It was nearly ten before she got to bed last night, and she's not used to keeping such late hours."

"It's only just after eight now, and her tutor doesn't come in on Sundays, which means she can sleep in as long as she wants tomorrow, so what's this really all about, Moll?" Hilda had eyed her narrowly. "Are you ashamed because I used the wrong knife to butter my bread?''

''Oh, Momma, as if I care about that!'' At her wit's end, Molly had rested an elbow on the table and clapped a hand to her forehead. ''If you must know, I've had about all I can stomach of Alec Livingston's smirking face, and as for the Cordell entourage at the next table…!''

''What've they done to us, beyond minding their own business and leaving us alone to enjoy ours?''

Was her mother really so naive that she couldn't read what lay behind the glances directed their way? Or notice how, when Molly caught them in the act, the older women in particular quickly lowered their eyes and allowed superior little smiles to accompany remarks uttered with such undisguised amusement that a person would have to be both blind and stupid not to recognize it?

She didn't care for herself. She'd been hurt and humiliated often enough before and lived to tell about it, but it broke her heart to have her mother and daughter ridiculed. So when Ariel had come back into the dining room and, at Dan's urging, skipped blithely over to speak to him, Molly's maternal instincts, already tuned in on high, switched to red alert.

Just one disparaging word, she'd thought, returning in full measure Yvonne Cordell's offended glare, *just one sneer, you despicable old witch, and I'll rip your throat out!*

Unaware of the drama being played out behind his back, Dan had poked a playful finger in Ariel's ribs and said, ''So how's the sore throat today, pumpkin?''

She giggled and caught at his hand. ''All better. It was better the next morning.''

Say ''Thank you,'' Molly tried to telegraph, her heart

hammering. *Don't give them the chance to tell you have no manners.*

But Ariel wasn't in receiving mode. "You're nice," she said, leaning trustingly against Dan's knee. "If I get sick, will you make me better?"

"I sure will, sweetie," he'd promised, tucking her braids behind her shoulders and picking a loose hair off her dress as casually as if he'd been doing it all her life. "Anytime you need me, I'll be there. You make sure you remember, I'm only ever as far away as a phone call."

The adoration in the gaze Ariel turned on her father had struck a fateful blow to Molly's conviction that she could pull off her deception. Already, with only a moment here and there snatched in passing as they went about their separate business, Dan and Ariel had connected like two magnets, and unless something was done to break it, the bond between them could only grow stronger.

Unable to tolerate another minute of the whole bizarre dining experience, she'd called out, "Ariel, come along, please. We're leaving."

"But, Mommy…!"

"Right now, Ariel!" Past caring that the brittle ring in her voice and the edge of hysteria in her behavior was raising eyebrows at the Cordell table, Molly jumped up, grabbed her purse and spun her mother's wheelchair away from the table so abruptly that Hilda's neck snapped back with the suddenness of it.

"How was dinner?" Dan had asked mildly, as Molly trundled her cargo past.

"Not up to my expectations!" she snapped, and fairly raced the wheelchair across the room.

"Leaving so soon?" Alec Livingston snickered as she approached the door.

"What does it look like?"

"I was hoping you'd stick around until things quieted down some and we could have a bit of a chat."

"I can't imagine that we have anything to talk about."

He'd shrugged his beefy shoulders. "I don't know about that, Moll. You and I go back a long way. Why don't we meet for a drink some night before I start work? We could catch up on each other's news and I could show you pictures of my wife and kids. I married Lexie MacGregor, in case you didn't know. Remember her?"

Indeed, yes! The eldest of nine, with carrot-red hair, freckles, eyes so pale a blue they were almost colorless and a permanently runny nose, she'd been the bane of Molly's existence in grade school. Heaven help the off-spring of such a couple!

"Bring any pictures of *your* husband with you, Moll?"

"None that I care to share with you," she said, the malice behind his question not escaping her. "Charge our meal to Suite 104, please."

"So it's a suite these days, is it?" he'd leered, feigning awe. "A far cry from Wharf Street, I must say, but it's nice to see that bagging a few bucks hasn't changed you. You're still the same old Molly Paget, despite it all."

And to think she'd deluded herself into believing she could outrun her past!

The couple on the TV screen clung together in a dark-ened house, horrified gazes trained on a body lying on the floor. Creepy organ music swelled in the background, and it took Molly a moment to realize that the repeated knock-ing she heard had nothing to do with the story being en-acted but was coming from the door to her suite.

Robe swirling around her bare feet, she crossed the small foyer and, not caring that she sounded about as wel-coming as the matron of a women's penitentiary, barked, "Yes? Who is it?"

"Bellhop, ma'am. Floral delivery for Ms. Paget."

"I didn't order flowers."

"Courtesy of management, ma'am."

Why would management send her flowers at this time of night? Skeptical, she peeped through the spy hole in the door and found the view in the corridor outside blocked by a huge bouquet of stargazer lilies. Reassured, she slid back the dead bolt and opened the door. "Put them over there," she said, gesturing to the hall table set against the far wall of the foyer.

"Sure thing." The voice belonging to the face hidden behind the flowers dropped from near falsetto to baritone. "Then after that, you and I are going to sit down and have a little talk."

It was the second time that night that a man had wanted to engage her in conversation against her wishes. The pity of it was, this time it wasn't Alec Livingston who'd disguised his voice to con his way inside the suite, and they weren't Alec Livingston's shifty little prune-pit eyes regarding her unsympathetically as she realized how easily she'd been duped into opening her door.

They were Dan's, and the uncompromising light in their clear blue depths left her quivering with agitation.

"Shouldn't you be somewhere else?" she said, with as much poise as she could muster, given that he was stalking her across the foyer with the unwinking concentration of a starving cat pursuing a mouse. "Such as dancing attendance on that rather pretty woman sitting next to you at dinner and whom I assume is your fiancée, given the size of the diamond she was wearing and the fact that she couldn't keep her hands off you?"

"I made my excuses," he said, his gaze never wavering. "She understood."

"Did she really? Would she also understand if she

knew you'd abandoned her to force your way in here and spend time with a woman you used to sleep with?''

"I didn't force my way in. You opened the door of your own free will and invited me in.''

"You deceived me.''

"The way you're trying to deceive me, Molly?''

A more loaded question was hard to imagine. Though it probably wasn't medically feasible, she felt as light-headed as if all the blood in her body rushed to her feet. Her heart pumped frantically, trying to restore order out of internal mayhem. Her palms grew clammy with sweat. Her tongue stuck to the roof of her mouth. "Tried to deceive you how?''

"By lying to me about Ariel.''

"Lying?'' she repeated, desperately playing for time. *Above all else,* the tiny voice of self-preservation cautioned, *do not let him trick you into making rash disclosures!* Swallowing, she wet her lips with the tip of her tongue and said hoarsely, "I have no idea what you're talking about!''

He had her backed into the corner by then, and loomed over her with one arm braced against the wall, barring any attempt she might make at escape. "Then let me spell it straight out for you, Molly,'' he said. "I have reason to believe I'm that child's father.''

Terrified, she stared at him, willing herself to wake up and find this was all a bad dream, that he hadn't confronted her with the one truth she was most anxious to hide.

On the TV, the organ music rose to a crescendo. A thin scream echoed. Thunder crashed.

"Well,'' Dan asked implacably. "Am I right?''

"No!'' Mutinously she glared at him, clinging to the one thing keeping her afloat: he could suspect all he liked, but he knew nothing for sure. "Whatever made you think she is?"

"You did. With every word and gesture. You never used to be afraid of me, Molly. Why are you now, when I've done everything in my power to set your mother back on the road to recovery? What is it about me that makes you want to take Ariel and run as far and as fast as you can, just to keep me away from her?"

"You've had too much to drink! You're imagining things."

Grasping her arm, he pressed his fingertips firmly against her inner wrist. "I'm not imagining the way your pulse is racing out of control, or the sweat beading your upper lip, or the outright terror glazing your eyes. I know a panic attack when I see one."

"I'm not interested in playing doctor with you, Dan. I outgrew that when I was seventeen."

He let go of her and laughed softly. "Come on, Molly, 'fess up! Or would you prefer I get a court-ordered DNA test to prove Ariel's mine?"

"Don't you dare! I will not have my child dragged through the courts to satisfy some harebrained notion that you've concocted for God only knows what reason!"

"Very noble of you, I'm sure. Pity you're not as high-minded when it comes to depriving her of knowing her father."

"She doesn't need a father!"

"Oh really? Has she ever said that? Or are you just imposing your views on her because of the screwed-up relationship you had with your own father?"

Beleaguered on every front, she cried, "Why are you doing this? Isn't it enough that you've always got every-thing else you ever wanted, without having to have my child, as well? If being a father's that important to you, go back to your fiancée and make your own babies, and leave mine alone!''

''Oh, Molly!'' With a tenderness which undid her more thoroughly than if he'd continued to hound her, he pulled her into his arms and stroked his hand soothingly up the length of her spine. ''I didn't come here to frighten you, my lovely, and I'm not trying to coerce you. I just want the truth.''

My lovely, he said, and it destroyed her.

He used to call her that when she lay naked beneath him on a deserted stretch of beach, or in a field, with only the moon to watch what they were doing. Drowsy with passion, his eyes would roam over her. And then his hands, and then his mouth, until she was quivering all over, beside herself and begging for him to come into her.

It wasn't fair that with two words called up from a past she longed to forget, he could undo her again so completely!

''Well, you *are* coercing me!'' she wept, her defiant bravado dissolving into tears of pure frustration. ''And what I don't understand is, why? Why do you even care about the truth after all these years?''

''Because it's never too late to fix past mistakes,'' he said quietly. ''And because it matters. *She* matters. If I'd known at the time that you were pregnant, I'd have taken care of both of you then.''

''We don't need you to take care of us, not then and not now. We manage very well by ourselves. I'm a good mother, a good provider.''

''And I'm her father.'' He nudged under her chin with his knuckles, forcing her to meet his gaze. ''Aren't I, Molly?''

This was how it must feel to be lost in a maze: to run

Get FREE BOOKS and a FREE GIFT when you play the...

LAS VEGAS

GAME

7

Just scratch off
the gold box with a coin.
Then check below to see
the gifts you get!

YES! I have scratched off the gold Box. Please send me my **2 FREE BOOKS** and **gift for which I qualify.** I understand that I am under no obligation to purchase any books as explained on the back of this card.

306 HDL DUYK   **106 HDL DUYZ**

FIRST NAME   LAST NAME

ADDRESS

APT.#   CITY

STATE/PROV.   ZIP/POSTAL CODE

(H-P-03/03)

7	7	7	Worth TWO FREE BOOKS plus a BONUS Mystery Gift!
🍒	🍒	🍒	Worth TWO FREE BOOKS!
🔔	🔔	♣	TRY AGAIN!

Offer limited to one per household and not valid to current Harlequin Presents® subscribers. All orders subject to approval.

The Harlequin Reader Service® — Here's how it works:

Accepting your 2 free books and mystery gift places you under no obligation to buy anything. You may keep the books and gift and return the shipping statement marked "cancel." If you do not cancel, about a month later we'll send you 6 additional books and bill you just $3.57 each in the U.S., or $4.24 each in Canada, plus 25¢ shipping & handling per book and applicable taxes if any.* That's the complete price and — compared to cover prices of $4.25 each in the U.S. and $4.99 each in Canada — it's quite a bargain! You may cancel at any time, but if you choose to continue, every month we'll send you 6 more books, which you may either purchase at the discount price or return to us and cancel your subscription.

*Terms and prices subject to change without notice. Sales tax applicable in N.Y. Canadian residents will be charged applicable provincial taxes and GST. Credit or Debit balances in a customer's account(s) may be offset by any other outstanding balance owed by or to the customer.

BUSINESS REPLY MAIL
FIRST-CLASS MAIL   PERMIT NO. 717-003   BUFFALO, NY

POSTAGE WILL BE PAID BY ADDRESSEE

HARLEQUIN READER SERVICE
3010 WALDEN AVE
PO BOX 1867
BUFFALO NY 14240-9952

NO POSTAGE
NECESSARY
IF MAILED
IN THE
UNITED STATES

frantically in one direction after another, seeking a way out, and instead keep coming up against a solid brick wall.

Suddenly defeated, she wilted against him and closed her eyes. "Please understand, I can't do this anymore tonight," she said, barely recognizing that pale, uncertain voice as her own. "Please...*please* go away!"

"Okay," he said, releasing her. "I'll go."

"You will?" For a second, perhaps two, a wave of delirious relief swept over her. She'd outmaneuvered him. She'd won!

"For now," he said. "But I'll be back."

"Why? What's the point?" She was pleading, unraveling before his eyes all over again, and damning herself in the process.

"Why do you think, Molly?" he said grimly. "To get to the truth. So I'll see you tomorrow and—"

"I'm busy tomorrow."

"So am I. We'll make it the evening, after I'm done at the clinic."

"I have plans for the evening."

"You're a rotten liar, my lovely, but just in case you are telling the truth, unmake those plans. I'll pick you up at six. And if you're not here, I'll wait until you get back—all night, if I have to. I'm sure you don't want that, because who knows what I might say to Ariel or your mother, in your absence?"

"That's blackmail," she quavered.

He considered for a moment, then shrugged. "Yeah, I guess it is."

"So?"

"So I'll see you tomorrow at six. Don't keep me waiting." He dropped a kiss on her cheek, strolled unhurriedly to the door and let himself out of the suite.

* * *

To avoid any sort of confrontation in front of Ariel or her mother, Molly was waiting at the main entrance to the Inn when he drove up the next night, and hopped into his car before he had time to get out and hold open her door.

He took her to a small town about forty miles down the coast, to an out-of-the-way restaurant perched on sturdy wooden piles over the water. "We're less likely to be disturbed here," he said, pulling into the graveled parking area.

The clear weather had held, leaving the sky a mass of stars reflected like polka dots on the quiet surface of the bay. Farther out, fishing boats rocked gently at anchor. Candleglow glimmered behind the square-paned windows of the low shingled building. The scent of wood smoke undercut the sharp, salty air.

If she and Dan had been out on a real date rather than what promised to be an examination of discovery, she'd have found the rustic setting charming and romantic. As it was, she said, "Less likely to be seen by anyone who matters is what you really mean."

He pressed his lips together and flung her a sideways glance. "Let's try to keep it civilized, okay? If I didn't want to be seen with you, I wouldn't risk bringing you here. It's a popular place with a lot of people from Harmony Cove who want a change of scene."

No one would have thought so, judging from the few patrons inside. "It's usually quiet on Mondays," their server told them, showing them to a table at the back, overlooking the water. "Do you care to begin with a cocktail before dinner?"

"No," Dan said, before Molly could open her mouth. "Just wine with the meal. We'll have a salad, the lobster thermidor, and a bottle of Louis Latour Chardonnay."

He'd barely finished ordering before a busboy plunked

a loaf of oven-fresh bread and a dish of butter curls on the table. Seconds later the server was back, bottle of wine and ice bucket at the ready. Fuming, Molly waited until the ritual of tasting and pouring was over and the man had disappeared to take care of their dinner order, then leaned forward across the table.

"I'd have liked a cocktail," she informed Dan, less because she cared one way or another than because she resented his high-handed attitude. "And furthermore, I can speak for myself, so save your leave-everything-to-me-little-woman act for the future Mrs. Cordell. She might appreciate it. I don't."

"Too bad," he said, helping himself to a chunk of bread. "I'm not having you wind up hammered until we've sorted things out. If you're still of the same mind after we've come to some sort of acceptable arrangement, you can order whatever you want and get falling-down drunk for all I care."

"I'm talking about a glass of sherry, not tippling myself into oblivion! In any case, who appointed you my watchdog? I've managed to live a clean and decent life this far, and it'll take a lot more than anything you can throw at me to change that. And what do you mean by 'acceptable arrangement'? My present arrangement is more than satisfactory, thank you very much!"

Idly he swirled the wine in his glass and took a sip. "Not too many years ago," he said, his tone deceptively casual, "proving paternity was something of a hit-and-miss affair. Although it was possible to determine conclusively that a man was *not* the father of a child, the reverse did not apply. The closest lab tests came was to indicate the possibility that he *could* be the father—along with any number of other men who happened to have the same blood type."

"And I should care because?"

He lifted his head and fixed her in a gaze which was anything but casual. "All that changed with DNA testing, Molly. Now, we don't even need a blood sample. A sliver of fingernail will do, or a minute flake of skin. Or a hair. Any one of these is enough to pinpoint without question the identity of, say, a murderer, a body decayed beyond recognition...or the man who fathered a child."

With shocking clarity, a picture formed in Molly's mind, of last night, and Dan playing with Ariel's braids. Of him lifting a stray hair from her clothing—innocently, she was sure, but it served to impress on her how simple it would be for him to collect evidence, should she force his hand.

He was watching her closely, dissecting her expression. Noticing the flush warming her face, the stifled gasp she couldn't quite suppress. "Shall I go on, Molly," he asked evenly, "or are you ready to stop yanking my chain and be straight with me?"

She stared at her hands, clenched to white-knuckle tension in her lap. How to answer? What to say? There was nothing; no way out—and he knew it.

Quietly he said, "I'm not going to take her away from you, Molly, it that's what's eating at you. That's not what this is all about."

"Then what *is* it about?"

"Our dealing with the fact that we share a child. Don't ask me not to care."

"Care if you must!" she whispered past the lump in her throat. "Care enough to let us alone! And if you won't do that, think of how it's going to affect your life once word gets out. That woman you're engaged to—"

"Summer," he said. "Her name's Summer."

"All right, Summer. She seems like a nice person, a

kind, sensitive person. What's it going to do to her if you insist on broadcasting that you're Ariel's father? Or are you planning to keep it a secret and be one of those anonymous benefactors who set up trust funds for other people's children for no apparent reason?''

''If that was all I wanted, I wouldn't be here trying to chisel the truth out of you. I wouldn't need to risk being seen having dinner with a beautiful woman and giving rise to gossip neither of us wants or needs. I could, as you rightly suggest, simply set up an account and make discreet deposits from time to time without anyone being the wiser.''

''Then what *are* you proposing?''

''Damned if I've got the answer to that, yet,'' he said, as the server returned with their salads. ''Begin by telling Summer, I suppose. She has a right to know.''

''And if she ends the engagement because of it?''

''I expect she will.''

''You don't sound exactly broken-up by the prospect.''

''Summer is a product of her upbringing, and the only child of ultraconservative parents. I'm not fool enough to think this is something she'll easily take in stride. Marrying a man with an illegitimate daughter waiting in the wings is too far beyond the socially acceptable boundaries that make up her life for her to accept it with equanimity.''

''Even if that child lives at the other end of the country and isn't really a factor in your life?''

She was grasping at straws, and he knew it. Pushing aside his salad bowl, he subjected her to another disturbingly direct gaze. ''I do not plan to be an absentee parent, if that's what you're hoping, Molly.''

''Are you saying you're prepared to move to Seattle?''

"No. I'm hoping you'll decide to stay, if not in Harmony Cove, then in some other town close by."

"Rearrange my life to suits yours, you mean?" She didn't bother to mask her scorn. "And to think I was half-convinced you'd changed! But you haven't, at all. You're as self-involved now as you were the last time I got myself mixed up with you."

"I intend to get to know my daughter, and I intend for her not only to get to know me, but also to understand that I'm not just a family friend stepping in as a surrogate parent, I'm the real thing."

Churning with anger fortified by a healthy dose of fear, Molly flung down her napkin and shoved her chair away from the table. "Not that I expect for a minute that you give a damn, but I don't intend to sit here meekly while you spell out your demands without any regard for what I want."

"Running out on me isn't going to change anything, Molly," he said calmly.

"It worked pretty well for you when you decided you'd had enough of me, eleven years ago!"

"You were only seventeen, for Pete's sake! I had no choice."

"You have the audacity to tell me you were trying to spare my feelings?" She laughed bitterly. "Is that what you were doing when you had sex with me, as well? How noble of you!"

To her surprise, she'd found a crack in his impressive facade of respectability. "Don't call it that," he muttered, averting his eyes.

"Why not, Doctor? It's a perfectly acceptable description. Or would you prefer something more clinically correct, such as *copulate?*"

"Stop it! You know damn well there was more to it than that. There was…"

"Yes? Come on, Dan! You're the man with an answer for everything, so don't let me down now. I'm waiting with bated breath to hear how you're going to rationalize this one!"

"Sit down and stop making a spectacle of yourself," he ordered, his blue eyes shooting sparks.

The new and improved Molly Paget would never have created a scene in the first place. But he'd revived too many old feelings of inferiority; of being dismissed because neither her feelings nor her opinions had any worth.

"How's this for spectacle?" she hissed, seizing his wineglass and upending it on the sizzling plate of lobster thermidor the waiter had just set before him. Then, for good measure—and in the interests of not letting it go to waste, since she certainly wasn't going to drink it—she threw her own wine on top. Most of it, she noticed with grim satisfaction, splashed all over Dan's impeccably correct silk tie.

Beyond caring that she'd put on a floor show which would keep the whole place entertained for the rest of the night, she then swept up her purse and coat, and stormed out.

CHAPTER SEVEN

SHE got as far as the parking lot before he recovered his wits enough to throw a fistful of bills on the table, mutter an apology to the waiter, and give chase.

Closing in on her, he snagged her by the collar of her coat and swung her around to face him just as she reached his car. "You're insane, you know that, don't you?" he panted.

"Don't you manhandle me," she shot back, lashing out at him like some wild gypsy, with her gold hoop earrings swinging furiously below her night-black hair.

His legitimate outrage diluted by laughter, he said, "I should put you across my knee and paddle your rear end!"

"Try it, and you'll be even gladder you've got a daughter, because there won't be any more healthy little sperm swimming out of your gene pool!"

It was the kind of threat which cowed most men, leaving them shrunk into pitiful impotence. In his case, it brought about the opposite effect. The feel of her in his arms—alive, tempestuous, hot-blooded—sent a jolt of awareness blasting to his groin.

The moon had risen over the water, casting enough light for him to see her big dark eyes flaming with passion. He could feel the quiver of excitement pulsing through her blood, telling him she was as conscious of him as he was of her, and equally wanting.

Caught squarely between defeat and desire, he slammed her up close to his body and buried his mouth against hers. The taste of her, hot and sweet, took him back more than a decade, to a time when the frenzy of the moment was all that mattered. Even with the iron-hard grip of winter chilling the air, he could smell wild flowers in full bloom, and the smooth, exotic scent of sun-kissed skin.

Desire as raw and untamed as the Atlantic tides swept over him, robbing him of the discipline and moderation he thought he'd perfected, and leaving him straining against her with the unashamed, unchecked fervor of a teenager.

She hadn't bothered to do up her coat. With rough impatience, he pushed it open and found her breasts, her hips, the alluring cleft between her thighs. She was wearing wool, a dress with a soft, full skirt which molded willingly to her shape. Beneath, silk slithered over her skin, whispering an invitation no red-blooded man could resist.

And all the time, her tongue danced with his, and she made little eager sounds deep in her throat, and she touched him as no one but she had ever touched him, skimming her long, clever fingers down his torso to cup him with deep and intimate knowledge. Toying with him until he thought he'd explode.

Teetering on the brink of madness, he lifted his head, searching for a place—a concealing corner of the building behind them, a boathouse, a heap of lobster traps, *anything* that would shield them from view—and found only the inhospitable remains of late-winter snow and a neat row of cottages lining the lane leading down to a small fishing pier at the other end of the bay.

"There's a motel," he began hoarsely, a flicker of memory conjuring up the image of a long, low building set amid a clump of white birch about a mile further down the coast.

"How long?" she said, reading his mind.

"Five minutes, if we hurry. Ten at the most."

"Take me there," she breathed. "Quickly…!"

Piling into the car with her and keeping one arm snaked around her in order not to lose the thrilling warmth of her body pressed against his, he sped along the twisting road. Ahead, perched on a jutting point in the next curve of the shore, the motel's red neon Vacancy sign shone like a beacon.

Engrossed in a TV sitcom, the clerk in the office barely glanced up as cash changed hands and keys slid across the counter. Equally impervious to anything but the urgency clawing at them, Dan hustled Molly into the blessed privacy of their assigned unit.

By then, cooler heads should have had time to prevail. The painful ache of arousal should have abated enough that he'd at least have exercised normal precautions. But enforced delay had merely sharpened the hunger, for her as well as him.

With the drapes drawn and the bedside lamp turned low, they tumbled onto the mattress, hands and mouths feverishly exploring…seeking…finding. Buttons and zippers snapped open, outer clothing lay discarded wherever it happened to fall. The touch of skin to skin, the musky fragrance of sex, the damp velvet petals of her flesh opening for him, were all that mattered.

Stripped of conscience and uncaring of consequence, his control held together more by divine intervention than anything a mere man could be expected to summon, he drove into her. Once, twice…strokes as deep and strong as eternity. And then, as the fine line between reason and madness scorched to oblivion, he thrust again and again, fiercely, furiously, lost to anything but the primal need to mate until, in a great blinding rush, he climaxed.

For long moments after, they lay together, bound by a tangle of limbs and the racing thunder of two hearts caught in the undertow of spent passion. The very atmosphere pulsed with heat.

At length he lifted his glance to the clock on the night table and because he felt he must, said, "It's late. I should take you home."

"Why?" she drawled huskily, her eyes gleaming, passion-dazed pools in the flushed oval of her face.

He'd been tempted plenty in his thirty-six years, but never in all that time had anyone seduced him with the utterance of one simple word sliding over his nerve endings like raw silk.

Stunned by the speed with which his body rose to the challenge, he crushed her mouth to his again, in a quick, hard kiss. Heard her sighing breath of reproach when he pulled away to strip off what remained of their underclothes.

Determined to show a little more finesse this time, he led her by the hand to the bathroom. Turning on the shower, he waited until the water ran hot, then pulled her with him into the stall and soaped her body.

She was beautiful all over. Despite the savage bite of winter, her skin retained the glow of apricots ripened in the summer sun. Her hips swelled sweetly below her tiny waist. Her bosom stood proud and firm.

Enthralled by her loveliness, he thumbed away the cloud of lather clinging to her breasts so that the dusky rose nipples lay bare to his gaze. "Did you nurse her?" he asked huskily.

"Yes," she sighed, her head falling back on a fracture gasp of pleasure. "Until she was nine months old."

"Was it an easy birth?"

"No. She was a forceps delivery."

He traced a finger over the smooth, flat contour of her belly and slipped it between her thighs. "I'd never have guessed. You're as tight as a virgin."

Letting out an inarticulate cry, she covered his hand and guided him to the swollen bud hidden between the folds of her flesh. "Touch me," she begged, as hot water cascaded around them. "Love me the way you used to, Dan."

Dropping to his knees, he parted her legs and found her with his tongue. She came almost immediately, her fingers knotted in his hair, her knees buckling, her body jerking spasmodically.

With the music of her cries still echoing around the shower stall, he reached up to turn off the water. Wrapping her in a towel, he carried her to the bed. "Again!" she whimpered, clawing at him as he flung back the covers . "Oh, please, Dan, again...now!"

"This time," he said, poised above her as she lay on the plain white sheet, "I will love you as you deserve to be loved."

A rash promise, he soon discovered! To touch her, to kiss her, to feel her quiver and undulate against him, and not be pushed to the brink, demanded more stamina than he possessed. Too soon, he was inside her again, with her long, lovely legs wrapped around his waist and her mouth blooming under his.

Her body clenched with the first faint tremor of orgasm. Trapped in a rhythm too hypnotically alluring to withstand, he moved with her and let ruthless nature have its way.

She contracted around him again, gave a sharp, delirious gasp, and arched beneath him in a series of wrenching shudders. And he was lost, finished, any notion of prolonging either her pleasure or his slipping beyond his grasp.

The distant thunder of completion spiraled to a roar and swept him beyond all the recognizable landmarks by which he charted his existence. Just then, and for the first few moments following, he could have died a fulfilled and happy man.

But life had a cruel way of surging back, of reminding a person that for every action, there was a reaction; for every stolen pleasure, a guilty price. As his blood slowed and sanity reclaimed its rightful place, he rolled to one side and stared at the ceiling.

A terrible heaviness filled his chest; the kind he felt when a patient came to him for help he was powerless to give. Some things couldn't be undone, and what he'd let happen that night was one of them.

As though she sensed his thoughts, Molly turned her head and looked to where he lay beside her. "Well, Dan," she said softly, her gaze fixed on his face, "where do we go from here?"

It was the sort of direct and justified question he'd learned to expect from her—and one for which he couldn't begin to formulate a response, at least not yet. Too much had happened in too short a time. Big, life-altering stuff. And he needed to come to terms with it before he shot off his mouth.

He started to tell her so, but she'd seen his hesitation and correctly interpreted its cause. "I guess I just got my answer," she said stiffly. "Thanks for nothing!"

"Don't presume to read my mind, Molly."

"Why not? It's an open enough book. Tell me, was a roll in the hay for old times' sake worth what it's now costing you?"

"What just happened had nothing to do with old times,

and you know it. Tonight was about the here and now. About you and me. And it's not something I can slough off as being of no reckoning. But nor was it something I had planned, so don't ask me to give you pat solutions until I've had time to process the ramifications.''

"Oh, shut up!" she spat, leaping off the bed and scrambling into her clothes. "Save your mealymouthed bafflegab for someone who cares."

"You care, Molly. You'd never have come here with me if you didn't. You wouldn't have kissed me the way you did, and you sure as hell wouldn't have let me kiss you, let alone make love to you."

If she'd discovered she'd just had sex with a troll, she couldn't have looked more disgusted. "Then more fool I! I guess I'm one those people who never learn."

More fool both of us, for ever having deluded ourselves into believing we could spend time alone and keep our hands off each other, he thought gloomily.

Whatever it was that had drawn them together in the first place had lost nothing of its appeal. Neither the passage of time nor the sobering effects of maturity and life experience could weaken its force.

It was all she could do look at herself in the mirror and not vomit. When was she going to learn?

The pitiful fact was, she never would. And if there had ever been any doubts on that score, she'd laid them to rest with a vengeance. To have fallen under his spell again, when she already knew the hefty price for making such a mistake! To have gone with him to a motel!

Two near-sleepless nights had gone by since then, and still her face burned at the memory. He hadn't even used a credit card to secure the room. Just like any other man sneaking around behind his wife's back—even if, technically, he wasn't yet married—he'd left no record of the transaction. Had probably signed himself in as Joe Blow, if truth be known. Cash and anonymity for a tumble between the sheets with a woman who'd never be good enough to be seen on his arm in public, but who could rev up his engines in ways his ultraconservative fiancée didn't dream existed.

"There are names for women like you," she whispered at the face staring back at her in the bathroom mirror, "and they're not pretty. Try 'slut' on for size, and see how you like the fit! Or 'whore'—that one's got a nice old-fashioned, hell-and-damnation ring to it. Your father would like that one, Molly Paget. He'd consider it custom-made for you."

"Mommy," Ariel called out, pushing open the door, "you've got a phone call."

Praise heaven! Any diversion was better than dwelling on this latest disaster. "Who is it, sweetheart?"

"Auntie Elaine. She said to tell you she's just checking in and that you made a bundle, whatever that means."

"She's talking about the last quarter's profits, sweetheart," Molly said, and hoped that was the only bundle in question, since, yet again, she and Dan had gone at it like frantic rabbits in the motel and forgotten about contraception.

"Oh." Ariel regarded her solemnly. "Are you sad, Mommy? You look sad."

She looked like a walking corpse! Would that she was as impervious to pain as one! "I'm just tired. I got home very late the other night, and still haven't caught up on my sleep."

Stop being such a damned fool and get in the car! Dan had bellowed, cruising beside her as she tramped down the deserted road.

I'd rather walk barefoot over red hot coals.

For crying out loud, Molly, it's below freezing out here and we're miles from home. Use your brains for once!

I think we've established I don't have any. If I did, the need for this conversation wouldn't have arisen in the first place.

You're asking to catch pneumonia.

No way. I'm not giving you another chance to maul my chest!

He'd muttered something under his breath—an obscenely graphic reference to what they'd just done in the motel room—and slammed the car to a stop. *Trying to talk reasonably with you when you're in this mood is a waste of time,* he'd said, grabbing her behind the knees and slinging her over his shoulder as if she were a sack of potatoes.

She'd have kicked him. Done lasting and excruciating injury to his precious crown jewels, if he hadn't caught her by surprise. But by the time she'd reached that stimulating conclusion, he'd literally stuffed her in the back seat of the car and taken off again at such dangerously high speed that, for once, she'd let discretion have the last word.

Revenge, she'd decided, could wait for another day. The odds of winding up mutilated in a mangled wreck, just for the pleasure of reaching over and throttling him with her scarf, weren't worth the risk, even if it was no less than he deserved!

"I'll speak to Auntie Elaine in here," she told Ariel, flopping down on the bed. "You go hang up the phone in the sitting room and when I'm done, we'll order whatever you want for breakfast from room service."

She lifted the receiver and could have wept at the sound of Rob's mother's voice, coming as clearly across the miles as if she were only next door. How many times over the years had Molly turned to her for advice, for help, for consolation? And how differently might her life have turned out if Elaine hadn't been the personnel manager who'd interviewed her for the big Seattle department store where'd she'd taken her first job after running away from home?

"I miss you, Elaine," she said, after they'd covered all the business they had to deal with. "And I miss Rob."

"We all do, my lamb, but that's not the only reason you sound so low. It's Dan, isn't it?"

Molly let out a hopeless sigh. "You know me too well."

"Have you fallen for him all over again?"

"It's worse than that. He knows about Ariel."

"I'm not surprised. When you told me he was your mother's doctor and coming in and out of the house pretty much at will, I had the feeling the secret wouldn't remain secret for very long, and I have to say, Molly, I don't see that as necessarily being a bad thing."

"You don't know the half of it!"

"I can guess," Elaine said drily. "I haven't known you all this time without picking up on the fact that you never got him out of your system. But you were a girl before, and he wasn't much more than a boy. You've changed since then, and you have to give him the chance to show you that he's changed, too."

"Some things—some *people* can't change."

"He's a doctor when you never thought he'd amount to anything but a playboy with no morals and more money than sense. He's working out of a cash-strapped clinic and on call pretty much seven days a week when he could just as well join a practice where someone else picks up the slack every time he feels like playing golf or partying.

So don't tell me people can't change because he's proof that they can. And you owe it to my sweet Ariel not to run away again until you've explored the wider dimensions of your relationship with him.''

"It's not that easy, Elaine.''

"I didn't say it would be. The issue is whether or not Ariel's worth the trouble of finding out if the dynamics of who you and Dan are can work, this time around.''

If only Molly could be as sure! "Days like this, I'd give a lot to be on the receiving end of one of your hugs,'' she said, forcing the words past the lump in her throat. "I'm scared, Elaine.''

"Don't make me laugh! You've got great instincts and more guts than any other ten people I know. Trust your feelings, my lamb. They won't let you down.''

The compassion and wisdom which made Elaine such a beloved friend, plus the strength which had helped her survive a broken marriage and the pain of losing her only son to AIDS, came across the phone line now, loud and clear. Only she could have spoken so bluntly and still be heard.

Within seconds of her call ending, the phone rang again. As soon as Molly identified herself, Dan's voice cut in.

"Don't hang up on me,'' he warned.

Chilled by the unfamiliar edge in his voice, she said, "I wasn't planning to.''

"That's good. I want to see you, Molly, some place private. There are issues we have to settle and I don't want to be disturbed until we've reached agreement on how to go about that.''

"If you're talking about a motel room again—!''

"I'm not. So if you're concerned I'm going to try to jump you the minute we're alone, you're worrying for nothing. I never mix business with pleasure—and this meeting, I assure you, is all about business.''

''All right,'' she said, despising the little stab of regret his assurance created. ''Where and when?''

''Anytime after five this afternoon. Where is up to you.''

''I was planning to stop by the house later on. We could meet there. It's private enough.''

And safe. Even Dan Cordell couldn't tempt her to forego moral rectitude in that place, not with her father's ghost lurking in every corner!

''Fine,'' he said brusquely. ''I'll see you there between five and a quarter after.''

He was late by nearly half an hour. Half an hour during which she fought the demons of disappointment hounding her as she paced back and forth in the living room, waiting for the sound and sight of his car pulling up outside.

''You took your time getting here,'' she greeted him, when at last he showed up.

''You took your sweet time opening the door,'' he shot back, rubbing his bare hands together briskly. ''Man, it's colder in here than it is outside.''

''The furnace doesn't work properly. That was another reason I moved us to the Inn.'' She swung back down the hall to the kitchen. ''We can talk in here. It's the warmest room in the house.''

''Don't suppose you've got any coffee on hand?''

''No.''

He shrugged and took a seat at the table. ''Didn't think so.''

He was wearing what she'd come to think of as his working clothes: blue jeans, navy crew neck sweater over white T-shirt, and sheepskin-lined denim jacket. Eyeing him surreptitiously, she decided he looked even more worn out than she felt. "Bad day?"

"The usual. We've had a rash of emergencies pile up on us. I've managed no more than about three hours' sleep in the last twenty-four." He yawned and glanced at her briefly from under his lashes. "The night before wasn't much better, though for different reasons."

"I haven't been doing all that well, myself."

"So it would seem. You look like hell."

Oh, terrific! Before he launched into a detailed description of just *how* she looked like hell, she took a seat on the other side of the table and said, "So let's settle whatever this pressing business is, then hopefully we can both go home and get some rest."

Fanning his long fingers wide, he spread his hands on the tabletop, and stared at them. "I suppose I should begin by apologizing for...betraying your trust the other night."

"And how did you do that?"

"I took advantage of you when you were emotionally fragile."

"Oh, spare me, please!" she said scornfully. "I'm as much responsible for what happened as you are. You didn't force me into anything I wasn't willing to go along with. If you owe anyone an apology, it's your fiancée. She's the one you betrayed."

"Summer and I are no longer engaged."

"Oh," she said. "And whose decision was it to call things off?"

"It was mutual."

"You don't sound as if it was. You sound miserable."

He passed his hand over his eyes and shook his head. "I'm tired. And I don't enjoy hurting innocent people." Glancing around, he said irritably, "If you don't have coffee, is there nothing else in this house? I could use a stiff drink.''

"Is that wise? What if you're called out on another emergency?''

"I won't be. I'm taking the next five days off. It'll be the first real break I've had in over six months, and I'm ready for it.''

To feel sympathy for him was dangerous. To note with concern the dark smudges under his eyes and parentheses of fatigue curving the corners of his mouth, foolhardy in the extreme. She couldn't afford to be vulnerable to his pain. She couldn't afford to care. Let him suffer!

"There's probably some brandy in the house. My father kept a bottle in his sock drawer, strictly for medicinal purposes," she said. "Will that do?''

Something which passed for a smile crossed his face. "Sure, as long as it doesn't taste of socks.''

Although they'd moved to the Inn only a few days before, already the upstairs held the dank, cold air of a house abandoned. Containing a shiver, Molly pulled open the top drawer in her father's dresser.

His socks were lined up in neat rows, exactly as she remembered them, and at the back a three-quarter full bottle of cheap brandy. Ever since she'd been a little girl, she'd known that when he measured an ounce into a glass and knocked it back in one gulp, it was because the stump of his amputated leg was giving him grief. Sometimes, if it was really bad, he'd leave his artificial limb in the armoire and hobble up and down the stairs on crutches. Shockingly, a feeling close to pity for the man touched her at the memory.

Unwilling to acknowledge such an anomaly, she grabbed the bottle and was about to turn away when she noticed a small picture frame lying facedown in the bottom of the drawer. She picked it and turned it over to find it held a photograph of herself—except from the quality of the print, faded and spotted with age, and the clothes the woman wore, it clearly was someone else who happened to be Molly's double. Curious, she stuffed it in the side pocket of the bag of personal items she'd packed for her mother, tucked the brandy bottle under her arm, and rejoined Dan in the kitchen.

He'd fallen asleep in the chair, with his head resting against the wall and his legs sprawled out under the table. But although she moved quietly, he heard the clink of the bottle hitting the counter and jerked awake. ''Must have dropped off,'' he mumbled.

''So it would seem.'' Staunching the well of sympathy which persisted in leaking through her resolve to remain distant, she unscrewed the bottle cap. ''This is the best I can come up with,'' she said. ''And I know for a fact we don't have any brandy snifters, so I'm afraid you'll have to make do with a dime-store juice glass.''

''Thanks.'' His fingers brushed hers fleetingly as he accepted his drink. Even so slight a touch, she thought dispiritedly, was enough to stir within her a host of useless longings. ''Aren't you going to join me?''

''Yes,'' she said, even though, just seconds earlier, she'd had no intention of doing any such thing, deeming it wiser by far to retain a clear head. But she needed *some* fortification against his relentless assault on her heart, and nothing else presented itself.

''Here's to self-discovery,'' he said, raising his glass when she came back to the table. ''I've done a lot of soul-searching over the last two days, and reached some pretty drastic conclusions.''

She took a sip of the liquor and grimaced at the foul taste. ''Such as?''

"For a start, I discovered I was more in love with the idea of marriage, than I ever was with Summer."

"I'd never have guessed it from the way you couldn't keep your hands off each other at dinner the other night."

"Appearances can be deceiving, Molly. I'm deeply fond of her, I admit, but we've never known the kind of grand passion which...well, never mind about that." As if he'd caught himself on the verge of admitting something better left unsaid, he reined himself in and continued, "What it all boils down to is that we drifted into a relationship less because we couldn't live without each other than because we've known each other all our lives and we...suited each other. She wanted children, and a husband who fits a certain mold, and I could give her those things."

"And what about what you wanted, Dan?"

He gave a self-mocking shrug and took another mouthful of brandy. "Let's just say a man can find it lonely, coming back to an empty apartment every night. He reaches a stage where, after a bad day when he's lost a patient too young to die, or missed a symptom he should have caught while there was still time to treat a life-threatening disease, he needs the warmth and solace of companionship. I thought we could both make do with that. That it would be enough on which to build a marriage. I was wrong."

"Why? Because you turned out to be not quite as perfect as she'd expected?"

"No," he said. "Because learning I had a daughter made me take a hard look at myself and I didn't much like what I saw."

"Which was?"

"A man following the line of least resistance. I want Ariel to be proud of me. If I can't have her love, I at least want her respect. But she's too much your daughter to be impressed by a someone who compromised his professional integrity for the sake of a warm body lying next to him in bed every night.''

''I don't see what one has to do with the other.''

''Marrying Summer came with a price. Sooner or later, I'd have been expected to sell my partnership in the Eastside Clinic and join her father's practice. Henry's a very fine doctor, and there's no question that working with him would have brought me a lot of prestige. But my heart would never have been in it. I'd have been taking the easy way out. Making do. Again. And I think Ariel deserves a better father than that.''

If he'd been half as principled at twenty-five as he was at thirty-six, Molly would have rejoiced. But it frightened her now. ''And how is this epiphany going to affect Ariel?'' she asked with studied calm.

He stretched and took a turn about the kitchen. ''I want to do what's best for her.''

''And what do you see as being best for her?''

''Providing her with a stable home.''

Molly's apprehension intensified, spiked a flash of anger. ''She already has a stable home. With me.''

''I'm sure in many ways she has. But the fact is, you've got a warped idea of what fathers are all about. Chances are she's going to grow up reflecting your attitudes, whether or not you intend that she should, and that's not healthy.''

''If you think you're going to take my daughter away from me, you're delusional!'' she said, her anger spilling over into outright fury. ''I'll see you in hell first!''

''No need to fly off the handle, Molly,'' he said, all calm, sweet reason in the face of her utter disarray. ''I already told you I'm not interested in doing that. In any case, this isn't about which of us is the more deserving parent, it's about accountability. I didn't act responsibly when Ariel was conceived, but I'm damned if I'm going to repeat the sin by walking away from my obligations now.''

''What if I want you to walk away?''

''What you, or I for that matter, want isn't the issue. What matters is our child.''

''My stars,'' she said, dripping scorn, ''no wonder you're so tired! You must sit up half the night polishing your halo.''

''Oh, hell, Molly, I'm no saint. I proved that two nights ago.''

''At least we agree on something.''

''You weren't exactly a model of decorum yourself, my dear!''

To her chagrin, she blushed. ''All right, if you're not planning to sabotage my relationship with Ariel, what are you proposing?''

''Marriage, I suppose,'' he replied dully.

''You *suppose?*'' Unable to believe she'd heard correctly, she stared at him in outrage. ''I'm blown away by your unqualified enthusiasm!''

''Because you're thinking about yourself. Try for a minute to step outside the personal. Or if you must focus on what's in it for you, consider the advantages of being married to me.''

She rolled her eyes disparagingly. ''Like what?''

''Respectability, social prestige, money.''

The crack of her hand across his cheek registered before the fact that she'd actually slapped him. Stunned, she backed away. ''I'm sorry!'' she whispered shakily. ''Truly, Dan, I am *so* sorry! I've never hit anyone in my life before.'' Reeling with shame and shock, she stumbled toward the door leading to the hall, knowing only that she had to get away from the sight of the red marks striping his face where her fingers had struck. "Dear heaven, I'm no better than my father!"

Dan's arms came around her from behind and stopped her in mid flight. "You're nothing like your father," he said against her hair. "And nor am I. But I *am* going to insist on being a father to our daughter, and I believe it's in her best interests for us to get married."

"And in mine to get a leg up on the social ladder." She winced at the backlash of arrogance which suddenly showed through the layers of his latter-day humility. "You know nothing about me, about who I really am or what I've accomplished, yet you have the gall to suggest I'd be bettering myself by becoming Mrs. Dan Cordell."

"No. I was merely trying to point out the practical merits of the arrangement since you've made it clear that appealing to your emotions won't get me anywhere."

"How could it?" she said. "I don't trust you. You couldn't wait to hotfoot it out of town as soon as you grew tired of me, the first time we hopped on this merry-go-round. Not once did you stop to wonder if there might be repercussions to having unprotected sex with me. And when you came back and found I'd left Harmony Cove for good, you made no attempt to find out why. You just let out a huge sigh of relief and forgot I ever existed, so explain to me, if you can, how we're supposed to build a marriage out of that?"

"By working on it."

"Forget it!" She twisted out of his hold before he seduced her into ignoring what she knew to be true. "Don't let conscience drive you into a liaison of respectability with me. I'm never going to fit in your rarified stratosphere, no matter how much you coach me. I'll pick up the wrong fork, or worse yet, eat with my fingers, and make you the laughingstock of Harmony Cove's social set. So do us both a favor and crawl back to Ms. Debutante. And if she won't have you and living alone becomes more than you can handle, buy yourself a German shepherd or a golden retriever for companionship.''

''You seem to be overlooking one crucial factor, Molly,'' he said, stalking her across the kitchen and drawing her into his arms again. ''There's another side to our involvement which has nothing to do with convenience or conscience, and everything to do with the fact that the sexual chemistry between us goes a long way toward compensating for the other shortcomings our marriage would face.''

The sane part of her brain told her that ''compensating'' and ''shortcomings'' weren't the kind of words a bride-to-be wanted to hear. She wanted ''love.'' She wanted joy and orange blossom and lace; wedding cake and confetti and promises of happy-ever-after.

The other part, the one which turned to mush at his touch, had her leaning into him and indulging in daydreams based on nothing but lust. Heaven only knew what she might not have agreed to if there hadn't come a sharp rap on the back door and Cadie Boudelet's moon-shaped face peered in through the window.

CHAPTER EIGHT

"CAME to see why there are lights on in this kitchen when I know Hilda's not at home these days," she announced, barging through the back door uninvited.

"No need to be concerned," Molly said. "It's just me."

"You—and the doctor!"

Fully aware of the conclusions being drawn and the kind of rumors which would have the whole of Wharf Street humming for the next quarter century, Molly could have tried quenching the woman's insatiable appetite for gossip with an explanation. But then, so could Dan. Instead he stood there looking as worn-out as if he'd just gone ten rounds between the sheets with a nymphomaniac.

It was all the provocation Molly needed. Why bother trying to haul her reputation out of the gutter at this late date? It had languished there so long, it wouldn't be comfortable anywhere else. "That's right, Mrs. Boudelet," she drawled. "Just me and the doctor. Imagine that!"

"There were lights upstairs, as well."

"I know." She smiled, and tried to look thoroughly debauched. "I was in my mother's bedroom."

Cadie eyed the brandy bottle and the half-empty glasses with avaricious malice. "I just bet you were!"

Enough was enough! "And we'd like to get back to what we were doing, if that's all right with you. Is there anything else you'd like to comment on before you leave?"

"Just this," Cadie proclaimed, delivering her parting shot to Dan. "You're very well thought of in these parts, Dr. Cordell, but keeping the wrong kind of company can ruin a man's reputation faster than frying fish with Satan. It'd be a crying shame if anything happened to change people's fine opinion of you."

"Still interested in marrying me?" Molly inquired, after the door slammed shut behind the infernal woman.

"Of course. Why would you think otherwise?"

"Because what you just witnessed is nothing compared to what you'd have to face if I were foolish enough to go along with your proposition. The minute I came back to this town, I felt the resentment, the dislike, the judgmental blame that's hounded me for as far back as I can remember. Even you were ready to condemn me."

"And I soon saw I'd misjudged you, and changed my opinion. Maybe if you didn't work so hard to maintain the bad-girl image, others would be more inclined to give you the benefit of the doubt, as well."

"People here don't change, Dan, and they never forget. As far as they're concerned, I'm still the same shameless creature who did nothing but add misery on top of misery to John Paget's life, and him with only one leg to stagger around on, poor man! I'm the delinquent daughter who didn't show up for his funeral, who left her mother to languish alone in hospital, who came back to take care of her only at the behest of a social worker, and never mind that I had no idea there'd even been an accident in the first place."

"Everyone held me in pretty low esteem at one time, too, Molly, and rightly so. But they don't anymore."

"Because you're a man," she said bitterly, "and the same old double standard still applies. As long as he eventually shapes up and proves his worth, a man can be forgiven his sins—even applauded for them, because it's natural for him to sow his wild oats. How else can he be expected to get them out of his system? But once a bad girl, always a bad girl, and I don't think you're ready to deal with having that label attached to your wife.''

''I can take the heat if you can.''

''I don't need the aggravation, not when I've got a home and a lucrative business, not to mention friends and the respect of colleagues, waiting for me on the West Coast. So if you want to build a life with me and Ariel, do it on my turf and move to Seattle.''

''Move to…?'' He looked at her as if she'd suddenly grown two heads. ''Maybe I haven't made myself clear, a minute ago. *I don't want to leave the clinic.* I like it there. I think I'm doing important work, that people are benefitting from what I bring to their lives. Most doctors aren't interested in that kind of practice. If I were to leave, my partners would have a very tough time finding someone to replace me. Is any of this getting through to you?''

''Stop talking to me as if I've had a lobotomy,'' she snapped.

''So you *did* hear me, the first time around?''

''I heard you say you'd have had to give up your work at the clinic if you'd stayed with Summer, because marrying a society princess exacts a price. What I hear you saying now is that with me for a wife, you're marrying down, so staying at the clinic's no longer a problem.''

She'd tested his patience too far. His eyes turned flinty, his expression cold as stone. ''Your incessant whining's growing tiresome, Molly. Do yourself and everyone around you a favor and dump the excess baggage you've been carting around for the last twenty years or more. And while you're at it, drop the attitude, as well. It's old, it's tired, and it's toxic.''

"Move to Seattle."

"No. My work here is important to me."

"And mine isn't, to me?"

"I'm not qualified to make that judgment. I don't know what your work involves."

"But you feel qualified to judge *me!* You've determined I can't do a good enough job bringing up my daughter by myself, even though you seem quite delighted with the results I've achieved so far. You've decided to do me the enormous favor of marrying me. But you don't have the first idea of what I'm all about. What's more, you really don't give a damn. All you care about is coming across as the big hero charging to the rescue of the fallen woman and her bastard child."

He straightened his shoulders. Inhaled so deeply his aristocratic nostrils flared. "The child I will protect with every means at my disposal, including flattening the next person who calls her a bastard. I'll see to it that she grows up secure in her father's love and wants for nothing. But tell me why I should bother with a woman who so thoroughly enjoys denigrating herself that she won't even consider the benefits of marrying her child's father. What the devil can I bring to her life that would make up for her having to abandon her role of woman wronged?"

"Certainly not a marriage doomed to fail before it begins," she spat, pride refusing to let her admit there was more than a grain of truth in his assessment.

"You're right." With bone-deep weariness, he reached for the jacket he'd slung over the back of a chair and shoved his arms into the sleeves. "It *could* have worked, but only if we were both willing to try. And you, clearly, are not."

He was halfway to the front door, ready to walk out of her life a second time, before she found the courage to follow him and utter the one word she'd been afraid to mention before. "What would be the point, when we don't love each other?"

"I'm past the age where I think love is a cure-all for everything, Molly," he said, pausing with one hand on the door knob. "If it were, I'd be out of work. But other things can cement a relationship between an adult man and woman."

"Like what? Rolling around in bed in a cheap motel room?"

"No," he said. "Like working together for the betterment of someone else. Like learning to respect and value one another for something other than sex."

She turned her face aside, not wanting him to see how devastated she was by his words. Were the two of them so out of sync that he didn't realize all he had to say was that he wanted her—*her!*—and she'd fall into his arms without a moment's hesitation? Had the fire and passion which had seared her soul the other night, and branded his name forever on her heart, been something only she had known?

"If that were all it takes, then you're right. We might have stood a chance," she said stonily. "But you *don't* respect me, and that's the whole problem."

"I respect you enough to offer you marriage."

"No. You're prepared to *do the right thing,* and that's not quite the same."

"Perhaps. But I'm burning a lot of bridges in the process, and that ought to count for something. I've ended my engagement. When the time's right, I plan to tell my parents about Ariel because I refuse to keep her hidden like some dirty little secret. And I'm prepared to stand in front of a minister or a marriage commissioner with you, and to hell with what anyone has to say about it."

"And you'd like to do it very soon, right?"

"The sooner, the better. Tomorrow, if it can be arranged."

"I thought as much." Misery gaining the upper hand, she started to cry because although he was saying all the right things, he was doing so for all the wrong reasons. "Once I'm your wife, no one will dare say a word about your choice, because the Cordells are above reproach of any kind. But you're so hidebound by public opinion you'd never dare flout convention and be seen in public with me without a wedding ring on my finger to give me respectability."

"You think you know me so well?" he said grimly, unmoved by her tears. "Fine, let's make a deal. I'll take you out on Saturday night, and you'll wear something eye-catching, to make sure we don't go unnoticed. If, when the evening's over, you still think I'm just 'doing the right thing,' I'll back off. On everything. Including letting Ariel know I'm her father."

"And if I don't?"

"Then we'll renegotiate. In good faith this time."

She smeared her fingers over her face and dug in her pocket for a tissue to wipe her nose. "Is that a promise I can count on?"

"You have my word on it."

She was crazy to believe him. Crazier still to let her heart leap with hope. But she did both anyway, standing where he left her at the front door for long minutes after he drove away, and dreaming impossible dreams based on improbable what-if's.

What if she could make him fall in love with her? What if they got married and she made him so happy that he wanted to have another baby with her? What if she left Elaine to manage the Seattle shop and opened another in

Harmony Cove? Flaunted her success, so that people could see she hadn't married him for his money? Proved herself to be better than they all expected?

And what if he takes you to some hole-in-the-wall dive on Saturday, where the lights are so dim that he could be treating the bearded lady from the circus to dinner, and no one would know the difference? her bruised ego inquired. *Get a grip on reality, girl!*

When he phoned to tell her he'd pick her up at eight, she said she'd meet him in the lobby of the Inn. And he knew why. She didn't want him around Ariel, trying to weasel his way into the kid's affections. So he made an end run by showing up a good twenty minutes early and bribing his way past the front desk, armed with flowers for Hilda and a couple of books for his daughter.

He'd have liked his first gift to her to be something more memorable; something she'd have for the rest of her life, like a gold bracelet, or a locket. But he knew he had to tread carefully. She was ten, not two, and smart as a whip. When she learned he was her father, she'd have questions. He couldn't afford to give the impression he was trying to bribe her to accept him.

"I didn't know Mommy was going out with *you!*" she said, her face lighting up when she opened the door and found him standing in the hallway outside the suite. "She just said she had to go to an important meeting."

His heart ached at the sight of her, all long, skinny legs, flying braids, and big shining eyes. He wished he could swing her around and make her squeal by blowing kisses against her neck before she grew too old for that kind of father-daughter thing. "She does," he said. "A very important meeting with me."

"Well, she's not ready yet. She bought a new dress and

thought it was a bit too low in front, so she's sewing it up. But Grandma's in the sitting room, if you want to come in.''

''I'd like that. It'll give us a chance to visit.''

He was parked in the wing chair opposite Hilda's, listening to Ariel read to him from one of her new books, when Molly finally appeared. ''How did you get in here?'' she demanded, stopping dead at the sight of him.

''The usual way. Through the door,'' he said, aiming for a little levity, which was no mean feat, given that he just about choked at the sight of her.

He'd always found her lovely, but tonight he saw that she'd learned to enhance her natural beauty by perfecting the art of elegance to go with it. She wore black, from the narrow dress which draped in folds of shimmery chiffon from shoulder to midcalf, to her sheer silk stockings and heeled pumps. Her hair was longer these days, curving almost to her jaw, so he couldn't tell if she was wearing earrings. Her only jewelry appeared to be a plain silver band at her wrist and a diamanté buckle cinching the dress just below her breasts.

No one seeing her for the first time would have guessed she'd grown up on Wharf Street, or tried to earn a little extra cash by taking a summer job slinging hamburgers at The Ivy Tree. The woman confronting him with such suspicion now was top-drawer all the way.

''I did *not* expect to find you making yourself at home in here,'' she said.

''He wanted to give me my present,'' Ariel explained, dancing over to show her. ''Look, Mommy, this one's a book about a girl with the same name as mine, and this one's got puzzles and stuff in it.''

''And he brought me flowers,'' Hilda chimed in.

Molly's glance slid past the books, and the bowl of

tulips on the coffee table, and came to rest witheringly on him. "So I see. Well, if you're quite finished distributing largesse, Doctor Cordell, shall we go?"

She dropped a kiss on her mother's head, and bent to wrap Ariel in a hug, then stalked to the door, rejecting with an abrupt tilt of her shoulder his attempt to help her put on her coat.

"Just what the devil do you think you're up to?" she snapped, the minute they were out of earshot.

"Taking you out for a night on the town, my lovely," he said. "Just as we planned."

"Don't play Mr. Innocent with me, Dan Cordell! We arranged to meet in the lobby, and you know it."

"I happened to be early and didn't see the harm in coming to the suite."

"And I suppose you just *happened* to come bearing gifts for my daughter and mother, as well!"

"No," he said candidly, steering her outside to his car. "That part was planned. And before you get your knickers in a knot, let me point out that I gave Ariel a couple of books, not a copy of her birth certificate with my name written in the space where her father's name should be. And why you'd begrudge your mother a simple flower arrangement when it's likely the first she's ever received anything with a florist's bow attached, is beyond me."

She was caught between wind and water on that one. All set to fire back a reply calculated to put him in his place once and for all, she compressed her lips and made do with a toss of her head which sent her hair fluttering around her face like glossy bird's wings.

Taking advantage of the cease-fire, he put the car in gear and drove away from the Inn. Soon, they'd cleared the town limits and were speeding north along a road cut through a sprawling birch forest.

Finally, her voice rife with another load of suspicion, she said, "Where are you taking me?"

"To Le Caveau, of course. If a guy wants to be seen, where else does he take his beautiful date on a Saturday night?"

He'd caught her by surprise again, except that this time her mouth fell open instead of snapping closed. Le Caveau was not just any run-of-the-mill restaurant, and she knew it.

Situated on the banks of a slow-flowing river some twenty-five miles outside Harmony Cove, and built along the lines of a French château, with thick plaster walls, vaulted ceilings and planked oak floors, it was famous both for its fine wine cellar and outstanding menu.

He was pretty sure it was Molly's first visit, but if she was overwhelmed by the massive grandeur of the place, she didn't let it show. When they arrived, she swayed ahead of him into the dining room as though to the manner born, inclined her head graciously as the maître d'hôtel showed them to a table on the edge of the dance floor, and looked around with utter composure while Dan examined the wine list.

"Champagne all right with you, Molly?"

"Lovely, thank you," she said, permitting herself a small, self-possessed smile.

"Any particular label you prefer?"

"I'm rather fond of Bollinger."

"Vieilles Vignes '92?"

He was testing her, certain she'd pulled the name out of a hat without knowing the first thing about it, but she floored him by coming right back with, "No need to go overboard, Dan. A '92 Grande Année will do just as well."

That pretty much set the tone for the entire meal. She

didn't need the waiter to translate the all-French menu. She knew exactly what *Fondue de Chicons à la Bière* was all about, which was more than he did, and tackled the quail and truffles following it with seasoned nonchalance.

Covertly he studied her as the meal progressed, mesmerized by her grace. Wanting to touch her, to kiss her. But there was more to her than innate sex appeal. *You don't have the first idea of what I'm all about,* she'd said, and she was right.

"Tell me about your business," he said, when the polite small talk leading nowhere finally withered and died.

"I own a shop which sells quilted things—bedcovers, baby supplies, decorative items, that sort of thing."

"And you're successful?"

"I am now," she said. "But it was hard to get started. I worked out of my apartment to begin with."

"Why quilts?"

"Because it was the only thing I knew how to do which would let me stay at home with my baby." She looked at him across the table, her big, wide eyes reflecting the candle flame in the middle of their table. "I had no other skills. I never finished high school. But I learned to quilt at my mother's knee. Every woman on Wharf Street could turn her hand to it. It was how they passed the long winter evenings. As things turned out, it stood me in very good stead."

"It's a shame about high school, though. As I recall, you hoped to go to university."

"Being a single mother with limited resources tends to put an end to those kinds of plans."

"If I'd known, Molly, I could have helped."

"I didn't want you to know," she said. "In fact, I made sure you wouldn't by moving to the other end of the country where, by a stroke of luck, I found a guardian angel."

"The guy you married, you mean?"

"I never married, Dan," she scoffed, "and you know it. That was just a story my mother dreamed up in case anyone from Harmony Cove found out I'd had a baby."

"So who was this guardian angel?"

"The head of personnel at the department store where I applied for work when I first got to Seattle."

"A man?" He had no business being jealous, but it was eating holes in his gut, worse than acid indigestion. He could see it all: beautiful young girl, pregnant and alone in the big city; suave, smarmy employer pretending to be her friend and crawling all over her the first chance he got.

"No. His mother."

"Oh." The heartburn subsided briefly, only to flare up more potent than ever as another snippet of information nagged at his memory. "But he's the one who was there for you when Ariel was born?"

"Yes."

"Was he in love with you?"

"He loved me. There's a difference."

"Did he want to marry you?"

"No. He was gay."

"*Was?*"

"He died nearly two years ago."

"From AIDS?"

"Yes." She leaned toward him, her eyes flashing fire. "And I don't want to hear a word from you about Ariel growing up around 'someone like that,' or any of the other rubbish you heterosexual studs obsess about. Rob was the dearest, the kindest man I've ever known, and I adored him. And so did Ariel. And if you ever try to tarnish her memories of him, I'll make sure you never see or speak to her again!"

Totally stunned by her outburst, he stared at her. "For crying out loud, Molly, who's being insulting now? I'm a doctor. I've treated patients with AIDS. I've seen first-hand what a wicked disease it is, and if you think I'd wish it on anyone because his sexual orientation isn't the same as mine, you don't begin to know the kind of man I am. Nobody deserves the devastation or heartbreak AIDS metes out."

"Well, not everyone agrees with you."

"I know," he said, aiming to lighten the atmosphere. "That's why I'm here with you tonight, remember? To prove it doesn't matter what other people think. And I'm sorry I never got to meet your Rob. I owe him a lot for being there when I should have been and wasn't. How's his mother coping?"

"Better." Her voice softened, and the sweet, fond smile curving her luscious mouth made him wonder how he'd ever found the will to send her away all those years be-fore. "She keeps busy, and that helps. She manages the shop for me and looks after the books, and is always there if I need a sitter for Ariel, though I try not to call on her too often ever since a new man came into her life."

"She's not married?"

"Divorced. Her ex couldn't deal with a gay son. But I wouldn't be surprised if she decides to give marriage an-other try. Hugh's a wonderful man and they have a lot in common. His son died of AIDS, too."

Her compassion moved him deeply. She might be all sass and defiance on the outside, but underneath she was a fine, intelligent woman who deserved a better fate than the one handed out to her, and he was a moron not to have recognized it sooner. "Do you know how to tango?" he asked, apropos of nothing but the compelling urge to touch her.

"Of course," she said, looking at him as if she thought he'd benefit from a brain transplant. "Doesn't everybody?"

"I don't. Will you teach me?"

"That's not a tango they're playing, it's rock 'n' roll."

"I know," he said, laughing. "Wanna boogie?"

She lowered her lashes, then lifted them again with slow deliberation. "You're asking me to dance?"

"Yes."

"In front of all these people?"

"Yes."

"You know we're already raising eyebrows all over the room?"

"So let's give them reason to rise a bit more. Come on, Molly. That dress deserves to be shown off."

"I didn't think you'd noticed," she said, allowing him to draw her onto the dance floor and into the relentless beat of "Blue Suede Shoes."

"Oh, I noticed! And it feels as good as it looks."

He should have known she'd dance like a dream, graceful and uninhibited; that they'd move together with the same instinctive knowledge of each other that they made love: two bodies in perfect unison and not one false step to throw them out of rhythm.

"We're creating a scene," she warned him, after a particularly spectacular bit of footwork. "It'll be all over town tomorrow that Dan Cordell's giving up medicine to open his own dance studio with that dreadful Molly Paget."

But she was laughing as she spoke, and he was captivated by her vivacity. He'd made her angry and made her cry too often. But if they could learn to laugh together...

The music slowed, segued into "When A Man Loves A Woman," and when he held his arms wide in invitation, she moved into them without a murmur of objection. He pulled her close enough that her thighs molded against his and her breasts flattened against his chest.

"You were right about my mother," she allowed, murmuring the admission against his cheek. "I could tell she was thrilled about the flowers. And it was kind of you to bring those books for Ariel. The glamour of living in a hotel is wearing a bit thin and although she has a tutor come in five days a week, I think she's missing being in regular classroom."

"She needs to put down roots, Molly. A proper home and friends her own age," he pointed out, gambling on the fact that she seemed more receptive to him than she'd been before. "Children thrive on permanence and normalcy, we both know that."

She stiffened in his arms and stepped back a pace. "Is this your subtle way of telling me I'm neglecting her?"

"No," he said, pressing his hand in the small of her back until she melted against him again. "It's my not-so-subtle way of trying to find out whether or not you're willing to marry me."

"Oh."

"You know," he said, the fragrance of her skin and hair assaulting his senses and leaving him dizzy with desire, "if we worked as a couple as well as we dance, we'd make an invincible team."

"If being a couple was as easy as learning to dance—"

"I'm not suggesting it's going to be easy, Molly. I'm suggesting it's possible. And given the situation, that's enough to make it worth trying." He lifted his head and glanced around the room. "If tongues were wagging before, they're working overtime now. You have to agree I've lived up to my end of the bargain, so I think I'm entitled to ask you if you're prepared to take me up on my proposal.''

She turned her face up to his. "Not exactly," she said. "But I am willing to consider a compromise. I'll find a place here, something big enough for Ariel and my mother and me, while I take your proposal under advisement."

"And what about room for me? Or do I get to hang out in the garage and sneak over after lights out to neck?"

"There'll be room for you, too—if things work out between us. Until then, stay in your own place."

"Holy cow, talk about making a guy feel wanted!"

"We need to get to know one another on a different level than the one which got us into so much trouble in the past," she said virtuously. "And you need to win over Ariel. Until we've accomplished both those things, we can't make a sensible decision about marriage. For that reason, the 'necking,' as you so charmingly put it, goes on hold."

"Cripes," he moaned. "I might as well join a monastery."

"Those are my terms, Dan," she said. "Take them or leave them."

CHAPTER NINE

THE sun was well above the horizon when Molly let herself into the suite the next morning. "I was about ready to phone the police," her mother greeted her. "I've been up half the night, wondering where you were. You're lucky Ariel's still sleeping. I don't know what I'd have said if she'd asked why you weren't here for breakfast."

"If it puts your mind at rest any, I wasn't doing anything I can't tell her about, Momma. In fact, I plan to give her a full explanation, as soon as she's up. Before then, though, there's something you need to hear and you'd better sit down first. You're making such a good recovery that I'd hate to be the cause of a relapse."

"You're going back to Seattle." Clutching a fist to her heart, her mother sagged onto the sofa. "Now that I'm more or less back on my feet, I knew it was only a matter of time before you left, but oh, my Molly, it's given me new life having you and Ariel here, and I'm going to miss you something fierce."

"It's not about us going back to Seattle. It's about Dan Cordell."

"What about him?" Hilda looked hopeful. "Is he in love with you? Does he want you to stay here?"

"He wants me to stay here, but not because he's in love with me."

"Because he doesn't think I should be left alone, then. That's it, isn't it? He's worried I'll slip back into that awful depression if you leave. Well, Moll, if that's what's keeping you here, I don't expect you to—"

"It's not." She hesitated, searching for a way to cushion what she knew would be shocking news for her mother. Dan was Hilda's idol; a solid, upright citizen and the dedicated doctor who'd not only restored her to health but who'd been instrumental in reuniting her with her daughter. To learn he hadn't always been such a paragon of virtue would not be well received.

If there was a delicate way to phrase such a bald truth though, Molly didn't have the luxury of time in which to find it, not if she hoped to lay the groundwork for Dan's visit later that morning. "He's Ariel's father, Mom," she blurted out. "And he wants her to know it. He wants to be part of her life. That's why I'm staying. But for what it's worth, if I change my mind and go back to Seattle, I'll take you with me. You'll never have to manage on your own again."

She'd hoped the last point would soften the blow some but, as she'd feared, her mother couldn't seem to get past the first piece of news. "Dr. Cordell's Ariel's father?" She blinked disbelievingly. "I don't believe it! He seems like such a nice man."

"He *is* a nice man, Mom. He always has been."

"Not if he waited until now to admit what he'd done!"

"He only just found out that Ariel's his, and he'd probably still be in the dark if I'd realized the Dr. Cordell who signed the medical end of the social worker's report on you was Dan, and not his father."

But Hilda was still trying to digest the impact of the original disclosure. "You slept with Dr. Cordell?" she said, looking more thunderstruck by the second. "How often?"

"Often enough, obviously."

"When?"

"Well, when do you think, Mom? The summer I ran away. That's *why* I ran away."

"I always thought it was one of the local boys who'd forced himself on you and you were too afraid to tell."

"It was Dan, and I was more than willing."

"You were just a child. What was he thinking of?"

"He thought I was more than seventeen because I lied about my age. When he found out, he ended the affair. But that's ancient history. It's how I break the news to Ariel now that concerns me. I need your help, Mom. I have to do this right."

"Yes, I suppose you do. Well, it's going to be a shock, no matter what, but it seems to me you and he should tell her together." Hilda shook her head as if to clear away the cobwebs of incredulity clouding her thoughts and grasp the bigger picture. "If being her father's so important to him, why won't he marry you, Moll? Doesn't he think you're good enough?"

"He wants us to get married. I'm the one dragging my feet."

"Because of who he is?"

She nodded. "And because of who I am."

"Oh, child, you outgrew Wharf Street years ago. You don't have to be ashamed of who you are now."

That was more or less the gist of what Dan had said to her, many times over the course of the night. But old habits were hard to shed and for every reassurance he'd given her, the ghost of her father had answered with a rebuttal.

"There's something else," she said, the thought of her father reminding her. "When I was at the house the other day, I found a photograph of a woman who looks a lot like me. It was hidden at the bottom of my father's sock drawer. I meant to mention it before, but I've had a lot on my mind.''

Her mother nodded. ''That was Sara Anne. She was your father's twin sister.''

''Twin sister?'' Talk about all the ghosts falling out of the closet in one fell swoop! ''Well, with such a strong resemblance, I guessed she must be a relative of some sort, but I didn't know she was my aunt. Good grief, Mom, why didn't either of you tell me?''

''John never spoke of her. She was killed in a train accident going on twenty-five years ago, but as far as your father was concerned, she died the day she shamed him and his family by running off with a married man. Before that, she and John were very close, and it broke his heart when she took up with her fancy man. But you know how proud and stubborn he was, Molly. He never forgave her for what she did.''

Molly shook her head, as taken aback by her mother's news as her mother had been by hers just a minute before. ''How strange,'' she mused, ''that they both died in an accident involving a train.''

''I've often thought the same thing myself, and wondered if it wasn't God's way of bringing them together again. Poor John. He carried so much inside and wouldn't let anyone get close.''

Hearing the sadness in her voice, Molly said, ''Do you miss him very much, Mom?''

''Yes and no. He wasn't a happy man, and it's not easy being married to someone, knowing he isn't content. But I understood him, and we got along better in the last few years.''

''Once I was out of the picture, you mean?''

''He saw Sara Anne every time he looked at you, Moll. And he was deathly afraid you'd turn out like her.''

"Well at least I lived up to his expectations in one area!"

"Don't talk like that. In his own way, he grieved when you ran away, but you had to know him the way I did to understand that."

"He refused to acknowledge Ariel."

"Yes, he did. And he suffered for it. Many a time I caught him looking at the pictures you sent, but he'd never admit to it. If he'd lived and you'd come home with her, I think that little girl might have been enough to bring you and him to some sort of understanding."

"We'd never have been close, Mom. There was too much bad blood between us."

"But you might have found a way to forgive him and that would've been a good thing. If you could lay your father to rest in your heart, I believe you'd be able to let go of all that anger you're burdened with, and be a better person for it."

Although she didn't say much at the time, the advice stayed with Molly throughout the morning, popping unexpectedly into her thoughts at odd moments. Which was rather amazing, considering the momentous events unfolding around her.

Or maybe not. Maybe sitting down to tell Ariel that Dan was her father without casting blame on him or herself gave her a different perspective.

"It's not that he wouldn't have loved you when you were a baby," she explained, floundering to find the right answers to Ariel's questions. "It's that he didn't know about you."

"Why didn't you tell him, Mommy?"

"Because I didn't think he'd want to know."

"Why? Because he didn't like you?" Ariel straightened her spine stubbornly, reminding Molly so much of herself that she almost smiled. "If he doesn't like you, I don't like him."

"He likes me, Ariel. But at the time when you were still a baby, he and I weren't very close."

"I don't think that was very nice of him. Everybody else has a daddy when they're babies."

"It was my fault, sweetheart. I went away so that he couldn't find me, and that was a mistake. Parents *do* make mistakes, all the time, but they often don't realize it until much later. And then they don't know how to undo it, so they try to hide it."

Was that how her own father had felt? He'd never had much of a way with words, even at the best of times.

"Now that he knows he's my daddy, is he going to live with us?"

"No. At least, not for now. But he still very much wants to be a real daddy to you."

"How can he be, if he isn't even going to live in our house?"

"We're still working on that, sweetheart. We'll talk about it when he gets here."

"He's coming to see me?"

"Yes.

"Do I have to call him Daddy?"

I'm your father, Molly Rose, and if I ever hear you call me "him" in that disrespectful way again, I'll tan your hide!

I wish you weren't my father! You're mean and hateful.

Ah, girl, there are days when I wish I wasn't, as well. It's no picnic trying to do the right thing with a creature as willful as you.

"Not unless you want to, Ariel. But I think he'd be very honored if you found you could."

"I'll have to think about it," Ariel said, bouncing up

from the footstool and spreading out the worksheets left by her tutor. "I'll decide after I've done my homework."

"I'm sorry if she hurt your feelings," Molly told Dan, a couple of hours later, after Ariel, having made it all too clear that it would take more than two books and an apology to compensate for ten years without a father, had flounced into the bedroom. "I'm afraid she's a bit overwhelmed."

"Understandably. It's going to take time for her to accept me. I didn't expect a miracle."

Perhaps not, but he looked crushed nonetheless, and the devastation which tinted his blue eyes the color of thunder heads moved Molly to the brink of tears. "It's not fair that you have to prove yourself to her when I'm the one who's to blame. If I'd been honest with you in the first place, you wouldn't be in this situation now."

"You didn't feel you could come to me, Molly," he said grimly. "And for that I have to take full responsibility. Ariel's no fool. Just because we didn't spell out the circumstances preceding her birth doesn't mean she couldn't read between the lines. She feels I deserted you. And she's right. I did."

The bleak picture he made, standing at the window with one arm braced against the frame and his head bent, as if he carried the weight of the whole world on his shoulders, cried out to her.

"There's a vulnerability that goes hand in hand with being a parent, Dan," she said softly, coming up behind him and stroking his shoulder. "A child holds your heart in her careless little hands and can crush the joy out of it without even knowing the pain she causes. But Ariel's not a cruel or unfeeling girl. She'll come around, you'll see."

At her touch, he pivoted away from the window and

pulled her into his arms. "It's the pain I've caused everyone else that's destroying me," he mumbled into her hair. "You might forgive me and perhaps Ariel will, too, in time, but I doubt I'll ever be able to forgive myself."

"Stop punishing yourself, Dan. What's done is done. Parents are a work in progress. We can't change past mistakes, but we can learn not to repeat them, and that's what you and I have to focus on."

"You can't have made too many mistakes," he said. "Our daughter wouldn't have turned out nearly as well, if you had."

The door to the bedroom opened. "I'm getting very hungry," Ariel announced sullenly, looking decidedly taken aback at the sight of her mother wrapped in the arms of her new father.

"Never let it be said I can't take a hint," Dan replied, and how Ariel could resist his smile was beyond Molly. "There's a really neat restaurant on the other side of the lake. How about if I take you there for lunch?"

"Mommy, too?"

"Of course. And Grandma."

Ariel took a tentative step closer, obviously as afraid of being excluded as she was afraid of showing she cared. "Will you let me have French fries?"

"Ahem," Molly said, looping an arm around her daughter's shoulders. "I forgot to mention, when I was telling you what a wonderful daughter you have, Dan, that she's a born negotiator."

He smiled again, and this time so did Ariel, just a little. "Takes after her mother then, doesn't she?" he said.

"I think I'll quite like him after all," Ariel informed Molly, when she tucked her daughter into bed that night. "I might even love him. Do you love him, Mommy?"

Had she ever stopped? She'd thought so. For months at a time, years even, she'd been able to push him out of her mind. But she'd never forgotten him, and no other man had ever taken his place because there was no forgetting or replacing a man like Dan Cordell.

"Yes," she said, not only because it was true but also because she wanted her child to know she'd been conceived in love. "I always have. The mistake I made was in not bothering to find out if he loved me."

"Well, does he?"

"Yes," she said again, certain that, even if it wasn't quite the case, he'd shown he cared about her, and this was one of those times when a little white lie served better than the literal truth.

"Then I think it's okay to do what you said, and live here. As long as we get to visit Auntie Elaine."

"We'll visit lots, I promise."

"You'd better hurry up and find us a house, Mommy. Grandma said it's must be costing you an arm and a leg to live here."

"I will." She tucked the quilt more snugly around Ariel's shoulders and dropped a kiss on her cheek. "I'll start looking tomorrow while you're having your lessons with Mrs. Franks. Get some sleep now, sweetheart."

The real estate office wasn't her only stop the next morning. Once she'd explained her needs and received a list of potential rental properties, she drove to the little white church on the coast road.

The huge maples dotted around the graveyard were in bud, the sky a deep blue, the air clear as crystal and full of birdsong. Some of the headstones, moss-draped and dating back over three hundred years, leaned tiredly, their inscriptions worn from centuries of winter storms. The most recent ones stood at the end farthest away from the church, where the land sloped gently down to an old apple orchard.

Finding her father's didn't take long. A stone plaque with just his name, the dates of his birth and death, and a simple Rest In Peace, marked his place. Unlike so many other graves, there were no flowers at his, for with her mother incapacitated, who else would have brought any? So he lay in death no different than he'd been in life. Bleak and removed.

Baffled to find her vision blurring, Molly blinked hard. But the tears continued to form, swelling and sparkling like diamonds along her lashes. He had been seventy-five when he died; an old man with few friends and only his wife to mourn his passing.

It wasn't enough. Moved by the utter loneliness of the sight, Molly dropped to her knees in the cool spring grass, and traced a finger over his name.

He was a lovely man when we were first married, her mother had told her, that first night she'd come back to town. *Big and strong...but it killed something in him when he lost his leg....*

And then, only yesterday, *It broke his heart when Sara Anne took up with her fancy man... Poor John. He carried so much inside and wouldn't let anyone get close.*

"I'd have loved you, if you'd let me," Molly whispered brokenly, the tears splashing down her face. "All I ever wanted was a daddy who liked me. I'd have been so happy to sit on your lap and have you read to me, or tell me stories about the way things were when you were growing up. I wouldn't have turned away from you because you were crippled. I wouldn't have broken your heart the way your sister did. I'd have been the good girl you always wanted."

A slight movement to her left had her looking up in horror. She didn't want anyone seeing her there. But it was just a squirrel watching her with bright, inquisitive eyes from his perch atop a granite slab. Beside him, a shrub of some kind was just bursting into bloom; pale pink trumpet-shaped flowers, with purple centers.

Slowly she stood and brushed at the damp earth clinging to the knees of her wool slacks. Stepping carefully between the graves, she snapped a branch from the shrub, much to the disapproval of the squirrel which raced up the trunk of the nearest maple and heaped abusive chatter on her for vandalizing his territory.

Returning to where her father lay, she stooped and placed the flowering stem beside his burial stone. It was the first time she'd voluntarily given him a gift. That it was such a pitiful token didn't seem to matter compared to the knowledge that it came from her heart. She hoped that, wherever he was now, it gave him the same peace it brought to her.

She drove back to the Inn with the windows rolled down. The breeze sent her hair flying in disarray. It needed to be cut, but finding the time to fit a visit to a salon in between her mother's medical and physio appointments, taking Ariel to the library, keeping tabs on her business, and now house hunting, was no mean feat, besides which Dan had mentioned in passing that he liked her hair longer.

Her mother, who made no secret of the fact that she hoped to hear wedding bells in the near future, accosted her the minute she set foot inside the suite. "You were gone a long time. Were you with Dan?"

"No. I went to see the churchyard to make my peace with my father."

"Oh, Molly!" Hilda's face crumpled.

"I thought you'd be happy!"

"I am, child! I prayed you'd find a way to forgive him."

"And forgive myself. Sometime between leaving here this morning and coming back again, I lost a lifetime of resentment. You were right, Momma. It's time to let go of the past and move on."

"You're going to marry Dan!"

"No," she said, smiling at her mother's eternal optimism. "I'm going to find us a place to live. Say goodbye to Wharf Street, Mom. You're moving up in the world."

She searched for a house for almost a month without success, but the frustration of not finding the right kind of place was offset by the benefits of time spent cementing her relationship with Dan.

They learned about each other during those late April days; discovered what they shared in common and where they disagreed. He and Ariel grew closer, too, although he admitted privately to Molly that, when he confided to his parents that he had a daughter, his mother had not taken the news well.

Sometimes, the three of them would go off for a picnic, or take a ferry ride to another part of the state. Other times, he and Molly would find an out-of-the-way place for dinner, or take long quiet walks along empty, moon-washed beaches.

But not once in that time, despite the ever-present temptation and opportunity galore, did they make love. They stood by their agreement: no sex to cloud the issue of whether or not they could make a go of marriage.

Then, just before the first of May, when Molly was convinced she'd never find the kind of house she was looking for, a property became available. As a child, she'd dreamed of living in just such a house, with tall stone chimneys, and wide, deep windows looking out across Harmony Lake to the rolling hills north of town.

It was a home from another era, full of quiet corners and padded window seats. The rooms were spacious, the maple floors polished to a satin gleam, and both the kitchen and bathrooms recently renovated. Its owners, who'd been transferred to Switzerland at short notice, had left it furnished with lovely antiques and beautiful rugs. All she had to supply were personal items like sheets and towels and dishes.

If she'd drawn up a wish list for a fairy godmother to grant, she couldn't have improved on what she found.

"I'll take it," she told the agent, and signed a six-month lease on the spot, with an option to renew or buy at the end of that time.

"When do I get to see this palace?" Dan wanted to know when he came for dinner that night and heard Ariel's ecstatic account of the boat dock at the foot of the garden and the swimming float about twenty yards off-shore.

In truth, Molly was reluctant to show it to him. They'd had a bit of a spat a couple of days earlier and it had all started with the question of where she'd live.

"Let me help you find a place," Dan said when, after hours of fruitless searching, she'd despaired of finding anything suitable. "I know people here. I have contacts. And if you're concerned about the cost of rent, I'll help."

"No," she'd said, fearing that the more she allowed him to come between her and the obstacles facing her, the greater the temptation to weaken and accept his marriage proposal for all the wrong reasons. "Spend more time with Ariel, instead. You can always hang out in the suite, if you don't want to risk being seen in public with her.''

"I'm not ashamed of my daughter, Molly," he'd said, peeved. "You're the one who asked me not to broadcast the news that I'm her father until you decide if you're going to make the move here permanent."

"And you're the one who told me your mother was less than delighted to learn she had a granddaughter, though I suppose, if she were to be honest, she'd admit her real problem lies with me."

"I already told you, I'll deal with my mother and anyone else who tries to make trouble for you."

She'd sighed, exasperated. "Why can't you see that I don't want to stay on those terms, Dan? You proved a point by taking me to Le Caveau, and I'm grateful for it. Now let me prove my point."

"It being...?"

"I will not be tolerated because of my connection to you. If I'm to make a new start here, it has to be because of who I am today, not because of who I used to be or who I've got lined up to go to bat for me."

And all of that was true. But there was something else she didn't mention. Sticking by their decision not to give way to the physical attraction between them was driving her to distraction. She knew what would happen if she found herself alone in an empty house with him.

"You can't keep skirting the issue for ever, you know," he said, reading her mind with uncanny accuracy. "Eventually you're going to have to deal with us."

"I will," she promised. "Soon."

If she knew him as well as she thought she did, she'd have guessed he wouldn't settle for that. As it was, she was caught totally off guard the following Sunday when he showed up on the doorstep of her new home half an hour after she arrived with a load of supplies she'd bought the day before.

"Housewarming gift," he said, thrusting a flowering plant into her arms—and his foot in the front door before she could shut it in his face.

"You're supposed to be on call," she said.

"I know, Molly. That's why pagers and cell phones are so handy. They give a guy freedom to come and go as he pleases between emergencies. So smile and say thank you, because you need a man with muscle to move all those boxes in the back of your vehicle, and I'm here to offer mine."

She hardly needed him to tell her he had muscle. Even if she hadn't already seen him naked as a jaybird and discovered the fact for herself at delicious, tactile leisure, the golf shirt and jeans he wore bore out the truth of his claim.

Oh, yes, she needed a man, all right, and not just any man. She needed him. Always had, always would. Worse yet, the frankly sensuous approval in his gaze as he took in her loose-fitting green-striped shirt, old white capri pants and ratty straw sandals, toppled the self-protective barriers she'd worked so hard to maintain and left her quivering with shameless anticipation.

To disguise her sigh of defeat, she buried her face in the flowers and sniffed their delicate scent. "Thank you for these. They're lovely."

"So are you," he said, reducing her already sagging willpower to the consistency of melted chocolate with his slow, devastating smile. "Even dressed like that. But then, with a body like yours, you could turn combat boots and army fatigues into a fashion statement."

She smiled back and since it was clear he wasn't about to leave, opened the door wider. "I suppose you'd better come in."

"I thought you'd never ask," he said.

CHAPTER TEN

THE second the front door closed, she knew she'd made a mistake. The whole setting was too intimate, what with the stairway curving suggestively up to the bedrooms on the left side of the hall, and the fat-cushioned couch beckoning from the sitting room on the right—not to mention Dan, parked squarely between the two, regarding her quizzically as though to say, *Okay, Molly, now what?*

"Come see the back garden," she said, racing him through the kitchen and out to the safety of the back porch. "There's a huge sugar maple at the bottom of the lawn, and what looks like a small orchard on the west side of the property."

"That's what it looks like, all right."

"Yes," she chirped, wishing she didn't sound so much like a deranged sparrow. "Quite a change from Wharf Street, isn't it? By the way, I went back to the old house the other day, to collect a few more things for my mother, and ran into Cadie Boudelet. She was almost civil for a change, so I asked if she'd be interested in supplying quilts for the shop. She does very fine work, you know."

"No, I can't say I do. Cadie's talents have never piqued my curiosity." He slid his forefinger under the open collar of her shirt and traced a beguiling path along her collarbone. "Yours, on the other hand, stir me to untold enthusiasm."

It was all she could do not to moan aloud with pleasure. Striving to preserve what remained of her self-control, she squeaked, "Did I mention I'm thinking of opening a shop here?"

"No, Molly. You haven't said much of anything to me lately, except 'Mind your own business.'"

"I'm sorry if I've hurt your feelings. It's just that I've grown used to being independent and it's a hard habit to break."

"I can handle an independent wife," he said, trailing his hand up the side of her neck to toy with her earlobe. "In fact, that's the kind I prefer."

"Don't get ahead of yourself," she said, with about as much authority as a titmouse staving off a hungry cat. "I haven't yet said I'll marry you."

"Not in so many words, perhaps, but the body language..." He smiled lazily. "That speaks for itself. But you were saying something about setting up business here?"

"Right," she said, backing away before he put her mettle to the test by continuing his explorations. "I came across a darling little place which used to be a fudge and chocolate shop, with gingerbread fretwork along the eaves and a spindled porch in front, tucked away in a corner of the main square. You probably know the place, although I don't remember it from when I lived here before. Anyhow, Cadie seemed quite thrilled that I thought her work was good enough to sell and—good grief, Dan, what are you doing?"

"Checking your heart rate," he said, trapping her against the porch railing, then calmly unbuttoning her shirt and slipping it off her shoulders. "You're babbling, and you're hyperventilating and, as a doctor, I'm concerned."

"Have you gone mad? The neighbors will see!"

"Not unless they're spying on us through a telescope, in which case," he said, pulling her into the circle of his arms and kissing the base of her throat, "it'd be a shame to disappoint them."

Her skin puckered with anticipation and delight. A tremor ran through her, so powerful her knees almost buckled. "Dan, if you keep this up, you know where it'll lead."

"We both know. The difference is, I can handle it, whereas you don't seem able to."

"Don't be ridiculous! It's a bit late in the day for me to act the nervous virgin."

"Exactly."

"But we agreed on a cooling-off period so that we could focus on shoring up other aspects of our relationship."

"I know. And if you want me to stop what I'm doing now, I will. But I warn you, I'm getting tired of your stalling tactics."

"I don't want you to stop. That's the whole problem," she whispered, lifting her mouth to his. "I've missed you."

"Then what *is* the problem?"

"I'm afraid."

"Of me?" He stared at her incredulously.

"Not of you. Never of you! But when we make love, there's always this little voice warning me that it takes more than sex to hold a marriage together."

He dropped his arms and stepped away from her, the light in his blue eyes turning flat and cold. "What you're saying is, before we take this relationship any further, you want guarantees."

"I suppose I do, yes."

"Well, brace yourself for a news flash, sweetheart. In life there aren't any. Some things you have to take on trust. I can tell you the advantages of our being married far outweigh the risks, that we have every reason to make it work, and that we're as sexually compatible as any two people can ask to be. But until *you* believe it, I'm just spinning my wheels, and that's beginning to irritate the hell out of me.''

''I realize that.''

''I don't think you do,'' he said flatly. ''I'm not a man normally given to ultimatums, but I've got to tell you, I'm tired of being given the runaround. This past month, I've jumped through hoops trying to reassure you, and it's gotten me precisely nowhere.''

''A month isn't much, compared to the lifetime we're talking about.''

''I agree. But let's face it, we aren't talking about a run-of-the-mill marriage, either.''

There it was, out in the open at last, the one thing her rational self had known all along and refused to accept: that theirs was no idyllic love match, no matter how much she wished it were.

She'd thought that, if she allowed enough time for their relationship to grow in areas beyond the purely sexual, he'd come to want her for herself, and not for any other reason. She'd hoarded each moment of tenderness they'd shared, every second of silent understanding and spontaneous reading of each other's minds, and tried to make them add up to the happy-ever-after ending she'd been looking for all her life.

It hadn't happened. All those intimate dinners and drives in the country and quiet walks where the two of them did nothing but talk and get to know each other without any outside distractions, had been for nothing. She and Dan were chasing different dreams.

The realization struck a killing blow. ''What you're really saying is, we wouldn't be getting married at all if it weren't that we have a child together,'' she said, her voice thick with misery.

"I don't deal in 'if's,' Molly," he replied, unmoved. "And I won't even try to speculate how you and I might have ended up if Ariel weren't in the picture. She is, and that's what we're left to work with. To that end, you set out certain rules, and I've complied with them. Ariel and I have grown close. She's as ready to accept me as her father as I've always been to acknowledge her as my daughter. But you continue to shut me out."

"If you construe our not having sex as me shutting you out, perhaps we're both wasting our time trying to make this work!''

"I'm not talking about sex, and well you know it."

"Then what? Give me an example."

"Okay." He leaned against the railing and regarded her impassively. "Did you bother to consult me about which school Ariel should attend, come September?"

"You're a busy man. I didn't think you'd want to be bothered with details like that."

"That's a crock, and you know it! Sure, I'm busy. We all are. But I'll never be too busy to look out for my daughter's best interests. Yet against my better judgment, I've sneaked around corners to keep my connection to her under wraps until *you* feel the time is right to make it public."

"I'm trying to protect her, in case things don't work out between you and me."

"Bull! You're using her to shut me out of decisions which should be ours to make, not just yours." He flung out his hand to encompass the house and its sprawling old-world garden. "I backed off helping you find a place to live even though, if we get married, it's where I'll be living, too."

"Don't you like this house?"

"Yes. You struck gold, no question about it. Rentals on the lakefront with a full acre of land attached, not to mention water rights, seldom come available. To find one in this condition is rare. That's not the point."

All the lovely, warm fluttering pleasure she'd experienced just a few moments before disintegrated into trembling fear at the steely determination in his tone. "Are you regretting having proposed to me, Dan? Is that what this is all about?"

"No."

"Then what are you saying?" she asked, unable to control the quaver in her voice.

"I want an answer to my proposal, and I want it now. You've just run out of options, Molly. It's time to fish or cut bait, as they say in these parts."

"And if I don't?"

"Then the whole deal's off, and as far as I'm concerned, you can pack up and go back to Seattle. I'll pursue my paternal rights through legal channels, Ariel will become one of those bicoastal children who spend half their lives flying between mom and dad's separate homes, and you and I will maintain a civil long-distance association for her sake."

"If you can let me go that easily, you can't have wanted me very badly in the first place."

"Oh, I've wanted you," he said. "I still do. But I'll survive without you. What I won't do is continue this ridiculous charade of being nothing but a family friend. Like it or not, I've got a name and a reputation to uphold in this town. One way or another, word that I'm Ariel's father will eventually leak out. I won't compromise my self-respect or her sense of self-worth by not marrying her mother. You might still get a charge out of thumbing your nose at social convention, Molly, but I outgrew it years ago.''

"How noble of you!" she flared, too hurt and disappointed to care that she was resorting to the one thing she'd sworn she'd never do, and that was beg for his affection. "What a pity you couldn't find room in your holier-than-thou aspirations for the bit about falling in love with one's spouse!"

"Teenagers fall in love, Molly. Adults recognize it takes something less ephemeral to survive the rigors of marriage."

"It takes something more than indifference on the husband's part, too!"

"Did I say I was indifferent to you? No, I did not. Far from it. I can truthfully say I desire you more than any other woman I've ever met. I've never felt more alive, never more challenged to be the best that I can be, than when I'm with you."

"Because of Ariel." More beaten down than she'd ever felt in her life before, she stared blindly across the lake. "If she weren't—"

"I told you already, I don't deal in 'if's.' Ariel's an important factor in the equation, of course, but in this case, the sum *is* greater than the parts." His shadow crept up behind her. His hand warmed her shoulder, his breath stirred her hair. "I want the exhilaration of a woman who constantly surprises me. The stimulation of matching wits with her. The sheer arousal of fighting with her because the making-up will be that much sweeter. And only since you came back into the picture have I realized how misguided I was to think I'd ever have found any of it with Summer. Can't we start out with that, Molly, and just let the rest happen when and if it's in the cards?"

Could they? Was it worth the risk of investing in marriage now, for the possible return of love later? Could she love enough for both of them, and not grow old and bitter if the scales remained forever tipped against her?

Could she walk away from him? Live without him?

"Yes," she said. "We can do that. I'll marry you on your terms, Dan. You can make it official."

"We'll do it together." He pulled her back to lean against him, and she thought that as long as she had his strength to rely on, she could do anything he asked of her, and more. As long as she had him and Ariel, she had what she needed to deal with the future.

"I'd like it if you'd go with me to the annual spring dinner dance at the yacht club next Saturday," he said. "We'll break the news then."

"I've never been to the yacht club."

"You'd never been Le Caveau before, either, but you handled yourself like a pro anyway."

This would be different, though. Everyone at the yacht club knew him. He was part of that monied, upper crust of society which owned yachts and belonged to clubs. He would be among friends, and she would be the interloper. He'd be with his family. She'd be alone.

It shouldn't have mattered. But it did.

Hilda had made an amazing recovery, graduating from wheelchair to walker in record time, and even getting around under her own steam on occasion. But she'd never manage stairs again, and what to do with the old house had been a concern.

The problem was solved a couple of days before the yacht club affair when one of Cadie's married children had offered to buy the place, and it hadn't taken much to persuade Hilda to accept. So immediately after breakfast the next Sunday, Molly left her mother and Ariel at Wharf

Street to pack up those small possessions Hilda wanted to keep; then, declining their offer to help, she drove to the new house by herself to put the finishing touch to things there.

In truth, she wanted to be alone for a while. Ever since she'd agreed to marry Dan, events had piled one on top of another at such overwhelming speed that she felt like a juggler with too many balls in the air. She needed to retreat and regroup, and the house on the lake was the place in which to do it.

Immediately she stepped through the front door, the timeless serenity of a home at peace with itself for decades enfolded her. Sunlight filtered benevolently through the windows, filling the rooms with dancing golden warmth. In the kitchen, the azalea Dan had given her the previous weekend bloomed in a riot of hot pink flecked with scarlet. Reflections from the lake shimmered over the ceiling and bounced off the burnished steel of the coffee machine she'd bought.

A hundred small tasks demanded her attention, but the lure of a cup of good coffee, sipped at leisure on the back porch, was too tempting to resist. It had been a week from hell in some respects. Too full, too exciting, too uncertain.

But seated in one of the Adirondack chairs, with her feet propped on the railing, the hazy blue expanse of the lake spread out before her, and a mug of The Coffee Bean's best espresso blend laced with hot milk at her side, Molly finally felt the cumulative tension of the past few days drain away.

It had begun when Dan had asked what kind of wedding she wanted. "A quiet affair, with just your family and mine," she'd said.

But even quiet weddings required some planning,

though if it had been up to her alone, she'd have settled for a ten-minute civil ceremony involving no one but the two of them and a couple of witnesses dragged in off the street. But there was Ariel to think of and, as Dan had pointed out, while an elaborate affair would be in poor taste, it was important for their daughter's sake, to endow the occasion with some dignity and pomp.

"On top of which," he'd added, wreaking his usual havoc by stringing a row of kisses along her jaw, "this'll be your only wedding, Molly, so you might as well make the most of it."

They'd set the date for the last Saturday of the month, just two weeks away, and decided on a five-o'clock ceremony performed by a marriage commissioner in a private room at the yacht club, followed by hors d'oeuvre and drinks, the whole to conclude within a couple of hours.

In the next day or so, she'd take her mother and Ariel shopping for something to wear. The catering staff at the club would look after everything else: a few flowers, champagne on ice for the obligatory toasts, a selection of appropriate recorded music—not to herald the bride's entrance, but to disguise any awkward lapses in conversation which might occur as residents of the elite Lake Harmony Bluffs did their best to embrace a family from Wharf Street.

No elaborate cake cutting ceremony, no traditional throwing of the bouquet, no fuss. Sort of like the impending marriage. Plain and unadorned and somewhat unconventional.

In between breaking the news to her mother and daughter, looking after business, and squeezing in a meeting with Dan at the jeweler's to choose wedding rings, she'd had to prepare for the upcoming yacht club dinner dance.

Unlike her wedding, it *would* be lavish; even she knew

that, remembering from previous years the extensive coverage the event received in the local newspaper. But she couldn't justify spending the money on something elaborate to wear, not when she had a closet full of lovely clothes in Seattle. So she'd arranged for Elaine to courier a dress for the occasion, a designer creation in cream silk embroidered with gold, silver and burgundy thread which Molly had worn to the Hospice Ball the previous year. An inspired choice, as it turned out because, late Friday afternoon, Dan had met her here at the house and given her a ring, a delicate lovely thing of rubies flanked by diamonds in a platinum and gold setting.

It had been such an unexpectedly romantic gesture that she'd been moved to tears. "I didn't want to make you cry," he'd murmured, taking her in his arms. "I'd hoped to make you feel better about everything."

"You have," she'd sniffled, burrowing into his embrace.

She'd welcomed the feel of him, warm and solid and enduring; the scent of him, faintly antiseptic after a day in the clinic. And she treasured him in a way she hadn't before, not because he'd presented her with an expensive token of his commitment to their future, but because he'd cared enough to make the occasion special.

He'd already put in a fifteen-hour day and could have been forgiven for keeping things simple. Yet he'd gone to the trouble to bring roses and champagne, and a CD of romantic songs. Streisand's incomparable voice flowed out of the house, reminding them of "The Way We Were" as the two of them sat on a garden bench sipping wine and watching the sun go down.

She'd found it easy to be lulled by the moment, the setting, the ambience, and suddenly all the reasons for keeping him at arm's length had seemed silly and contrived. Whatever other problems they might be facing, there was one thing they'd always done well.

"Make love to me, Dan," she'd whispered.

Shockingly he'd refused. "I gave you the ring because I wanted you to have it, no strings attached. It's not intended as a bribe."

She'd run her hands over his long, lean torso. "If I thought it was, I wouldn't be trying to seduce you."

He'd put up a token resistance, but she'd seen the smoldering light in his eyes, felt the involuntary tremble in his body, and taken shameless advantage of it.

"It's been weeks since I've even kissed you properly," he muttered.

"I know," she said, offering him her lips. "And I think it's high time you rectified that."

Long, agonizing seconds elapsed during which his gaze toured her face, feature by feature, in the fading light. Delicious seconds, brimming with promise and exploding into a starburst of desire held too long in check when he finally brought his mouth to hers.

"Come with me," she whispered, when at last he lifted his head, and taking his hand, led him inside the house and up to the master bedroom overlooking the lake.

They'd arrived at a new beginning, in a place far removed from an anonymous motel on the highway. This room was where their real life together would start and she wanted their first time together there to be memorable, not blurred by haste or cheapened by stealth.

They made love in the big four-poster bed, on new sheets laundered in water scented with lemon-verbena, with the pale orange glow of sunset streaming through the windows and touching their limbs with gold. When at last he entered her, prefacing the moment with long minutes of exquisite discovery, she was hot and damp and quivering for him.

He moved, gliding within her in long, sure strokes. And she, caught in the rhythm of ecstasy and unprepared for the sudden rush of pulsing sensation racking her body, spoke aloud the words she'd never let herself utter before. "I love you, Dan," she cried.

He raised himself on his arms and looked down at her, and for one breathless second she saw something in his expression which left her suspended on the sharp edge of hope. Just fleetingly, at that moment of complete connection between them, she thought he might tell her he loved her, too.

He had not. He'd scrunched his eyes closed and with a mighty groan had driven into her one last time. She'd held him as he flooded her body with his seed, stroked his hair as he collapsed against her, his chest heaving. And not let him see the tears creeping down her face.

She wanted too much. She always had.

"We're going to be just fine together," he said, cradling her head on his chest later. "Everything's going to work out, you'll see. There'll be no bumps in the road that we can't handle, no unexpected detours."

Yet she hadn't been able to shake the sense that nothing was ever quite that simple or easy.

"You're just nervous about the dinner dance," he'd said, when she'd tried to explain. "Stop worrying. You'll do just fine."

In hindsight, she supposed he was right. The evening had, for the most part, been a success. No one had snubbed her. She hadn't spilled red wine over the person sitting next to her at dinner, or slopped béarnaise sauce on her dress.

News of the engagement had been received with subdued enthusiasm as befit such an occasion, given that Dan's former fiancée was among the guests. Dan's father had hugged Molly and quietly asked when he was going to meet his granddaughter. Mrs. Cordell, dressed to kill in gorgeous black lace and a choker of emeralds which would have made a jewel thief drool, had offered a cool cheek and said nothing at all, which was preferable to having her froth at the mouth at the idea of a Cordell marrying a Paget.

There'd been only one small fly in the ointment. Molly had returned from the ladies' room just after ten o'clock and found Dan had gone missing. He wasn't at their table, nor was he dancing.

Uncertain where to look and feeling conspicuously abandoned, she'd stepped outside to the deck overlooking the yacht basin. At first, it had appeared she was alone but the flutter of pale fabric in the shadows had drawn her attention to Summer, deep in conversation with him.

As Molly watched in stunned disbelief, he'd taken Summer by the shoulders and bent to kiss her, then drawing her hand into the crook of his elbow, turned and started back to the door. When he'd seen Molly, he'd said easily, "I was just coming to find you, my lovely."

She hadn't taken the incident well. Baring her teeth in a smile which she well knew more properly resembled a grimace, she'd waited until the elegantly poised, elegantly cool, elegantly everything Summer had swayed back into the ballroom, then turned on Dan and spat out, "If this is how you plan to behave as a married man, you can take your ruby ring and stuff it up your nose!"

He'd had the effrontery to burst out laughing. "Before you go off the deep end, let me explain."

"What's to explain?" she'd seethed. "Coming across

you sticking your tongue down another woman's throat is pretty self-explanatory, if you ask me.''

Another paroxysm of laughter had overtaken him. ''Honey,'' he choked, recovering himself with difficulty, ''a peck on the cheek hardly amounts to adultery. I was merely congratulating her on her new romance. In case you haven't noticed, she's glowing.''

The devil of it was, he *had* only kissed the woman on the cheek. It wasn't his behavior which was out of line, it was Molly's own—and she knew it as well as he did.

''I'm sorry,'' she'd mumbled, glad that the encroaching night hid her flaming cheeks.

''You should be,'' he said, still chortling. ''Come here, you idiot, and let me show you what having a tongue rammed down your throat really feels like.''

She'd gone willingly into his arms, and he'd kissed her with exquisite, heart-stopping tenderness. She would have died for him at that moment, if he'd asked her to.

''I'm really sorry, Dan,'' she'd said again, when she'd recovered herself. ''I guess I'm a little on edge.''

''I don't know why,'' he'd said, cupping her face. ''You're the belle of the ball.''

She wasn't. But if he thought so, that had been just fine with her.

Recalling the whole silly event as she hauled herself out of the chair and went back to the kitchen for a coffee refill, Molly knew a near disaster had been averted only by Dan's sense of humor. He was right. She needed to lighten up.

The doorbell rang just as she finished steaming more milk. Expecting it was Dan, who was on call again but who'd promised to stop by if he could spare the time, she turned off the espresso machine and went to let him in.

"It's time I gave you your own key," she began, opening the door with a flourish and a mile-wide smile.

But it was his mother on the other side, and Molly would have had to be brain dead not to know this was no friendly social call. Yvonne Cordell was a woman on a mission which had nothing to do with welcoming her future daughter-in-law to the neighborhood.

Formidably chic in pale green linen accented with a violet scarf, she fanned herself with her smart little leather purse and surveyed Molly from beneath the brim of her straw hat as if she'd come upon a deviant form of life hitherto undiscovered. Feeling nakedly indecent in her shorts and top, Molly stared back.

Finally Yvonne broke the painful silence. "May I come in?" she inquired, the eloquence in her raised eyebrows a trenchant comment on Molly's lack of manners.

"Of course." Belatedly Molly stepped back and did her best to resurrect the smile which had slipped into obscurity at the sight of her visitor. "But if you're looking for Dan, he's not here."

Yvonne swept through the hall and into the kitchen as if she owned the place, slapped her purse down on the breakfast bar and prepared to do battle. "I know. Which is why I am."

"May I offer you coffee?"

"No, dear. I'm not here to exchange recipes."

"I see."

"I doubt it, so let me blunt."

"Please do," Molly said, the lump of foreboding in her throat swelling to epic proportions.

Yvonne Cordell opened her purse and took out a checkbook. "How much will it take to persuade you to terminate this farce you've entered into with my son?"

CHAPTER ELEVEN

STUPEFIED, Molly stared at her. "I'm not sure I understand what you mean."

"I want you to go away, darling."

"Go away where?"

"Any place you like." Yvonne shrugged her elegant shoulders and took out a silver-capped pen. "The farther removed from this town, the better."

"You're actually asking me to end my engagement?"

"Precisely. And I'm willing to pay handsomely for your cooperation."

Struggling to absorb the shock, Molly sank onto one of the stools at the breakfast bar before her legs gave out from under her. "You're trying to buy me off?"

"Since we're speaking frankly, yes."

"Perhaps you've forgotten, Mrs. Cordell, that I have a daughter."

"I'll take that into account."

"She's Dan's daughter, too. Your grandchild."

"So you say. But that sort of claim is, I believe, one of the oldest tricks in the book when a woman of limited means sets out to attach herself to wealth." Pen poised, she arched her brows again. "Which is why I'm prepared to offer you generous compensation to remove yourself *and* your daughter from this town and leave my son to get on with the life he had mapped out for himself before you turned it upside-down."

"Does Dan know you're here?"

"Don't be absurd, Ms. Paget! He would be furious if he knew about our little arrangement."

"He might also be very hurt to learn that people he believed he could trust would betray him like this."

Yvonne Cordell scribbled in her checkbook, tore off the page and laid it face-up on the counter so that Molly could read the amount written there. "Count the zeroes. I think you'll find there are enough to buy your silence."

"My silence will cost you nothing because I wouldn't dream of telling Dan about this meeting. And not all the money in the world would induce me to stoop to the kind of abominable behavior you're suggesting. I'm afraid you've wasted your time, Mrs. Cordell. I am not for sale, and neither is my daughter."

"Of course you are, darling. Everyone is, if the price is right."

"In your circle of friends, perhaps, but not in mine," Molly snapped, anger foaming within her.

Dan's mother smiled. "From everything I hear, you have no friends, at least not here."

"Oh, I don't know about that," Molly said. "I doubt I'll have much trouble forming a circle of acquaintances at least as well connected as yours. I thought people treated me very warmly last night."

"Naturally. Because you were with Daniel. *He,* you see, belongs. You, on the other hand, are a misfit. Just because no one was so crass as to let you see what a fool you made of yourself, with your flashy dress and patently obvious attempts to appear at ease, doesn't mean they weren't laughing at you behind their hands. They were simply too well-bred to be obvious about it, that's all, besides which they'd never want to humiliate Daniel."

Molly was crumbling inside, shattered beyond repair by the woman's chiseling erosion of her self-confidence.

Laboring to remain calm, she said, "If that's true, I think they might also be well-bred enough to overlook my shortcomings and recognize something you seem determined to overlook, which is that I happen to love your son very much."

"Ah, but does he love you, Ms. Paget?"

The bottom fell out of Molly's world at that. Numb with pain, she groped for an answer which would at least win her the battle, if not the war, and found none. "I know he loves his daughter," she cried, "and she loves him. What kind of monster are you that you'd set out to destroy a little girl's future by depriving her of a father? Leave us alone, for pity's sake!"

At the outburst, a wrinkle of distaste crossed Yvonne Cordell's aristocratic features. "If you weren't so caught up in your own melodrama, you'd realize you're out of your depth. I play to win, Ms. Paget—*always*. So do yourself a favor and take the offer I'm laying on the table. Cut your losses and run. Buy yourself a nice house—on the West Coast. A nice car—on the West Coast. In other words, darling, face the facts. You don't belong here. You never did. They don't even want you in that dreary dockside area you call home. So do everyone a favor and take yourself and your benighted child out of our lives, because I promise you, if you persist in trying to hang on to my son, I'll make your tenure here a living hell."

She swept the checkbook and pen inside her purse, snapped the bag closed and adjusted the angle of her hat. "Oh, yes, and one more thing: the owners of this house and I are old friends. A phone call from me is all it will take for the rental agreement you've signed to be rescinded. When it comes to who wields the most power, money and connections always win out."

* * *

He knew something was wrong, the minute he stepped out of his car. For a start, the front door stood ajar and she was nowhere to be found, although her van was in the garage.

Not a man normally given to grisly imaginings, he couldn't repress the prickle of apprehension skittering up his spine at the unearthly silence emanating from the house. The *dead* silence.

Had she fallen from a stepladder and hurt herself? Broken her back or her neck? Had some unsuspected pervert infiltrated the community and finding her there alone, given in to uncontrollable urges? A rapist, a serial killer?

Possibilities so outlandish he couldn't believe he entertained them, spun in lurid Technicolor through his mind and left a film of cold fear on his skin. He raced up the steps and into the front hall, his yell splintering the indifferent silence of the afternoon. "Molly!"

It seemed he waited an eternity for a reply; an eternity comprised of a millisecond fraught with unbearable suspense. Shocked by the hammering insistence of his sixth sense which told him something had gone dreadfully awry, he charged through the house, beginning with the bedrooms, and then through the reception rooms and the library, dreading what he might discover.

Finding them undisturbed, he made his way through the butler's pantry and came at last to the kitchen. At first glance, everything seemed to be in order there as well, except for her unwashed coffee mug.

Then he saw her ring, and next to it the check, the obscene sum for which it was made out, and the signature. And his indeterminate apprehension crystallized into knowledge.

"Have you lost your mind?" his mother had practically shrieked, arriving on his doorstep that morning before he was properly awake. "Ending your engagement to Summer is one thing, but to leap into another with that woman…and to spring her without warning on your father and me last night, in front of all our friends!"

"*That woman* happens to be the mother of my child, Yvonne," he'd reminded her coldly.

"If you're so sure of that, why are you keeping it such a deep, dark secret?"

"Because Molly doesn't want the news made public just yet."

"Until she finds herself safely married to you, you mean! Good lord, Daniel, come to your senses before you find yourself saddled with another man's child and a woman who's using you to elevate herself to a position in society she could never achieve on her own merit!"

He'd had his share of run-ins with his mother over the years, some more acrimonious than others, but it had been some time since they'd squared off with so much vehemence.

"Butt out, Yvonne!" he'd warned her. "And while you're at it, button your lip around your friends because I won't tolerate a smear campaign against Molly or our daughter."

"And if I refuse, what then, Daniel?"

"Remember the last time you tried to bend me to your will, Mother? Let's see, how long was it that you neither knew where I was or even *if* I was? Two years? Three? Would you like me to show you again how effectively I can cut you out of my life?"

He'd seen the color wash out of her face and thought he'd driven home his point firmly enough for the matter to be closed. He should have known better. When it came to preserving what she perceived to be her elevated position in society, his mother's warped judgment ruled the day and, sadly, she possessed the tenacity of a pit bull in defending it.

Pocketing the ring, he went out to the back porch and scanned the expanse of lawn sloping down to the water. The rush of relief when he spotted Molly at the far end of the boat dock had him vaulting over the railing and striding down the path to where she sat facing the lake, with her bare feet dangling just above the water.

"Hey," he said, dropping down beside her and bouncing the ring on the palm of his hand. "What's this all about?"

She didn't answer. And when he looked at her, he knew why. He'd seen grief before, more often than he cared to count, but he'd never thought to see it etched so savagely on her face. Never thought to see her looking so pale and stripped of emotion that she might as well have been dead. And never for a moment expected to see her so devastated that the tears simply flowed down her cheeks in a silent, unending stream as if someone had turned on a faucet and forgotten to turn it off again.

This was not the Molly he knew, the one whose fire had stirred him to realize that, in order to find meaning in his life, he needed something more than the easy, undemanding pattern which had evolved with Summer.

The light had gone out, leaving behind a waif so lacking in substance that he wanted to shake her until the color surged back to her cheeks, and she raged at him for the injury he'd let happen to her.

At a loss to define the knot of emotion lodged in his gut, he put his arms around her and pulled her tight against him. He might just as well have tried to contain water in his bare hands. She slipped out of his hold and shuffled to the far end of the ramp, as if she thought he might contaminate her.

"Don't push me away, Molly," he said hoarsely. "Tell me what happened and let me fix it."

Her chest heaved in a massive sigh. "You can't fix it," she said dully, "because you can't change the truth."

"Whose truth are we talking about, angel?" he asked, a terrible aching filling his heart. "Yours, or my mother's?"

"Both," she said. "I thought I'd outgrown my past, risen above it. Fooled myself for years into believing it. Eventually, though, destiny catches up with a person. Mine caught up with me today."

"Stop it!" he raged, anger coursing through him bitter as acid. "Do not succumb to the poisonous influence of a control freak like my mother, please!"

"It's not just your mother. Everybody's been trying to tell me the same thing, one way or another, from the minute I set foot in town again—Cadie Boudelet, Alec Livingston. And you. Oh, you've been kind and decent and offered to make an honest woman out of me," she said, "but even you can't bring yourself to love me. How many times do I have to keep banging my head against the wall before I learn it's not going to change anything and the only person I'm hurting is myself?"

"Since when do you have to turn to someone else for validation, Molly, when you can look into your own heart and know that you're not to blame for other people's mean-spirited censure? Take pride in what you've accomplished. And recognize you've passed too far beyond the limitations of Harmony Cove for anyone to appreciate the strides you've made."

"Including you, Dan?"

"Oh, I'm beginning to get a glimmer of understanding," he said ruefully. "But for a supposedly intelligent man, I've taken a hell of a long time to see what's been under my nose for weeks. Give me your hand, Molly, and let me put this ring back where it belongs.''

"I can't," she said, her voice breaking. "I can't marry you. I won't have Ariel subjected to the scorn and insult I had to put up with when I was her age. I'm taking her back to Seattle where she'll be safe. You can visit her whenever you want. You'll always be welcome in our home. But please don't ask me to stay here, because I can't.''

He saw the set of her mouth, the determined angle of her chin. Even through the tears and despair, the strength which had elevated her so far above her disastrous childhood shone through, and he knew that, for now at least, he was wasting words trying to convince her to change her mind.

"Then do this for me instead," he begged. "Come back to the house. Take a bath, wash away those tears, and put on something from that closet you've already filled with clothes. By the time you're done, you'll be feeling much better and I'll have brought you proof that you're wrong to give up on us without a fight.''

She did as he asked because she was too empty to care one way or another, and too tired to resist. As if she were very old and frail, he lifted her to her feet and shepherded her carefully up the path and through the house to the master bathroom.

While the tub filled, he stripped off her clothes with a tenderness and care exceeding anything he'd demonstrated before, then disappeared downstairs, returning a short time later with a glass of wine which he set on a stool within easy reach of where she lay up to her neck in scented bubbles.

"Relax and try to enjoy," he said, dropping a kiss on her head. "I'll be back very soon."

In fact, he was gone over an hour. Expecting he intended dragging his witchy mother back to the house to force an apology out of her, Molly used the time to shampoo her hair and loofah her body to satin smoothness. Not that it would change anything, but he was right on one score, she admitted grudgingly, slipping on a silk caftan. A hot bath had made her feel better, although not to the point that she was willing to forgive the insults she'd suffered earlier.

Wineglass in hand, she drifted through the upstairs rooms, saying her good byes and wishing things could have turned out differently. She loved everything about the house, from its gracious proportions and sunny exposure, to the grand old maples and slender birches screening it from the property next door. But she'd been foolish to think it was meant for her. What use had she for so many bedrooms, or a nursery?

Such a place was meant to be filled with the sound of children's laughter, not the lonely footsteps of one little girl ostracized by her classmates because her mother wasn't "their kind of people."

It was almost dark when Dan's car turned in the driveway, followed almost immediately by another. By the time she reached the downstairs hall, he was in the front door and she saw with horror that he had Ariel by the hand and that his parents were close behind.

"What have you done?" she whispered, drawing Ariel away from him and into the protective curve of her body.

"I thought you'd like to see our daughter, my love," he said calmly.

"And her?" She jerked her head to where Yvonne Cordell stood proud and unrepentant next to her husband who had the grace to look woefully ill-at-ease. "Did you think I'd like to see her again, too? Isn't once enough for one day, Dan?"

"Don't upset yourself, angel," he said, the glance he spared the older woman so cold that even Molly shivered. "My mother isn't staying. She merely came to collect something she left behind this morning. And to explain to Ariel why she left it here in the first place."

For once, Yvonne Cordell seemed at a loss. Paralyzed, almost.

"Go ahead, Yvonne," her husband said grimly. "Explain why you tried to bribe our son's fiancée into taking our granddaughter and leaving town."

"I...made a mistake," she said.

"But if you're my grandma, why did you do it?" Ariel asked, gazing at her out of eyes so wide with puzzled innocence that Molly's heart shifted in her breast. "Don't you like me?"

Yvonne Cordell tried to meet her gaze, and couldn't. "Of course I do, dear."

"Try to sound as if you mean it," Dan advised her tersely.

Defeated, she lifted her head and stared at him. "You've made your point," she said, her voice cracking. "I was wrong. I'm sorry. I had no idea that...you and Ms. Paget...Molly...cared for one another so much."

"You don't know the half of it, Mother," he said. "I doubt you ever will. But if you're at all interested in knowing your granddaughter and any brothers or sisters she might one day have, I suggest you make a concerted effort to overcome your prejudice. Otherwise you will never see my family or me again."

"You don't need to hammer the point home, Daniel. I'm aware I've handled things badly."

"That's something, Yvonne," her husband said, "but it's not quite enough, is it?"

But Molly had been on the receiving end of humiliation too many times herself to enjoy watching someone else squirm. "Yes, it is," she said, pity overcoming her resentment after all. "Thank you, Mrs. Cordell. I know this isn't easy for you."

At first, Yvonne said nothing. She swung her gaze to the floor, raised it to the ceiling, and appeared to wage a fierce inner battle with herself. Then, clearly shaken, she stepped forward.

"No," she said. "It isn't easy because we come from different worlds. But I was wrong to suggest mine is better than yours. None of us has control over the circumstances into which we are born. It's how we choose to deal with those circumstances which divides or unites us." She stretched out her hand and rested it briefly on Ariel's head. "Sometimes it takes a child's clear thinking to point the way to finding that unity. But these are only words, Molly, and words are never enough. I hope you'll allow me the opportunity to back them up with action."

Much later that evening, after the senior Cordells had left and Dan had returned from taking Ariel back to the Inn, he and Molly sat side by side on the back porch with only a candle and the faint prick of stars to light the scene.

"Your mother's right, you know," Molly said, staring out to the black expanse of the lake. "Words, by themselves, aren't enough."

"Some words are," he said. "Words such as 'I love you.' They can be the most healing words in the world. I love you, my Molly."

"No," she said. "You feel sorry for me, and responsible for Ariel. But that doesn't add up to love, and your saying it does won't change my mind about leaving here.''

''Fine,'' he said. ''Leave, then. Run to the other ends of the earth, if you think it'll change anything. But it won't. I'll follow you. If Seattle is home for you, it'll become home for me.''

''You belong here, Dan. You're the jewel in this town's crown—the good doctor, the fine, upstanding man every eligible woman wants to marry.''

''I'm also a fighter. I've fought to save lives, to promote health, to care for the sick—and I'll fight to the death to hold on to the woman I love.''

''I'm not that woman,'' she said. ''You don't need someone like me. Your mother was right this morning. Public opinion matters.''

''You're *all* I need,'' he said, so fervently she almost believed him. ''And I don't give a rip about public opinion. You are what matters. What we share is what matters. I want to be your husband. I want to lie beside you at night and see your lush, beautiful mouth bloom with passion under mine, and those gorgeous eyes turn heavy with desire when I take you in my arms.''

''You don't—''

''Yes, I do!'' he said, with a catch in his voice. ''I want to feel your heart racing against mine. Make you pregnant. See you grow heavy with another child of mine. Watch you hold my son to your breast, catch your glance across a roomful of people and know that the message in it tells me you want to be alone with me. You were a little part of my past. I want you to be all of my future. I'm a better man because of you. I need you, Molly, and I do love you.''

She was sobbing before he was even half-finished. ''I want to believe you,'' she wailed. ''But I'm afraid.''

"Not you," he murmured, hauling her out of her chair and onto his lap. "Listen to me, my lovely. A man and a woman get together for a season, a reason or a lifetime. At first, with us, it was for a season. And I admit, when I first asked you to marry me, it was for a reason. But now, I'm asking you for a lifetime. You're my lodestar, Molly. You give me direction and purpose."

"Oh!" she wept, hiding her face against his neck as all the sharp-edged hurt washed away in a great flood of tears. "I must look such a mess!"

"No," he said, lifting her head so that his mouth hovered over hers. "Even now, you look beautiful because, to me, you don't know how to look any other way."

She could have drowned in the kiss with which he sealed those words. "I love you, Dan," she said, for only the second time in her life. "I always have. I always will."

"Then say you'll stay here and build a life with me. Marry me."

"Yes," she said, the very real possibility that happy endings were not just for other people finally coming home to roost. "Yes, on both counts."

He took her upstairs then, and made love to her. Brought her home to him in the most enduring way that any man can claim his woman.

"Eleven years ago I couldn't offer you anything," he told her. "This time around, I'm promising you forever."

It was all she'd ever wanted.

Him. Forever.

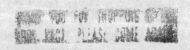

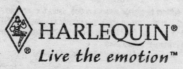

A "Mother of the Year" contest brings
overwhelming response as thousands of women
vie for the luxurious grand prize....

Kate Hoffmann

Jacqueline Diamond

Jill Shalvis

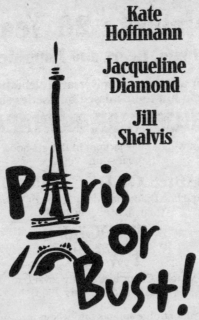

Paris or Bust!

A hilarious and romantic trio of new stories!

With a trip to Paris at stake, these women are
determined to win! But the laughs are many as three of
them discover that being finalists isn't the most
excitement they'll ever have.... Falling in love is!

Available in April 2003.

HARLEQUIN®
Makes any time special®

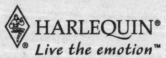

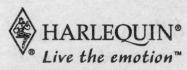

The world's bestselling romance series.

HARLEQUIN®
Presents

Seduction and Passion Guaranteed!

GREEK TYCOONS

**They're the men who have everything—
except a bride...**

Wealth, power, charm—what else could a heart-stopping handsome tycoon need? Find out in the **GREEK TYCOONS** miniseries, where your very favorite authors introduce gorgeous Greek multimillionaires who are in need of wives!

Coming soon in Harlequin Presents®

SMOKESCREEN MARRIAGE by Sara Craven
#2320, on sale May 2003

THE GREEK TYCOON'S BRIDE by Helen Brooks
#2328, on sale June 2003

THE GREEK'S SECRET PASSION by Sharon Kendrick
#2339, on sale August 2003

Available wherever Harlequin books are sold.

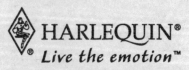

HARLEQUIN®
Live the emotion™

Visit us at www.eHarlequin.com

HPGTYC